My Most Memorable Flights

Flights

50 Years of Private Flying & Other Travels

BY RAMON N. ARCHER

iUniverse, Inc.
New York Bloomington

iUniverse books may be ordered through booksellers or by contacting:

iUniverse
1663 Liberty Drive
Bloomington, IN 47403
www.iuniverse.com
1-800-Authors (1-800-288-4677)

ISBN: 978-1-4401-8148-1 (sc)
ISBN: 978-1-4401-8149-8 (ebook)

Printed in the United States of America

iUniverse rev. date: 9/30/2009

Contents

FORWARD

Undoubtedly there are many pilots who have had similar experiences to John's, but it seems that many of his have been unusual, often outstandingly exciting and sometimes downright breathtaking. Flying private aircraft has been John's passion for more than fifty years and many of his more exciting experiences have been related in this writing.

John Archer was perhaps not a true pioneer of flying since his flying carrier began a few years later than the early barnstormers. He grew up in a small town in Montana where he began to fly light aircraft at an extremely young age. This was shortly after the end of the Second World War and he has continued to fly light aircraft for more than 55 years since. For most of us who have been active in flying in recent years, this makes him truly an early pioneer even thought his beginning was not at the time of the Wright brothers.

Over the past half century John has had more than the average exciting exploits in small aircraft which many have been captured in this writing.

Although predominately a series of events concerning flying of light aircraft, this writing is more than just about flying. Also related are events concerning John's travels as well as flights throughout America, Canada, Australia, New Zealand, Fiji and Hawaii. Along with travel logs of these countries, John has highlighted the strikingly different lifestyles witnessed in such places as the Outback of Australia, the backcountry of Fiji, and even the remote reaches of Hawaii. Interspersed are several cultural differences which were found by John to be most humorous, particularly between Australians and Americans. There are numerous accounts of actual flying episodes throughout many countries, ranging from enjoyable and exciting to suspenseful and gripping.

Enthusiasm for flying generated excitement for John and many of these moments have been passed along in this writing. John melded in some of the more exotic events of his travels that occurred throughout his flying carrier. It is anticipated that these episodes and odysseys will be as enjoyable to the reader as the doing has been for John.

EXCITING EARLY FLIGHT TRAINING

One of the first airplanes ever seen in the small community of Fort Benton, Montana arrived in 1938, more than 70 years ago. Fort Benton is the oldest city in Montana and the inhabitants there were use to horses and buggies and Model "A" Fords in those days, not airplanes.

The sight of this airplane was quite a remarkable departure from the ordinary. Not only was it one of the most unusual sights ever seen in this area, it was also one of the largest single vehicles to come to this small community. The entire population came from miles around to see this behemoth with wings.

The airplane sitting in the cattle pasture, later destined to become the local airport, had a corrugated aluminum body with a large engine on each wing. It was manufactured by The Boeing Company in Seattle, Washington. A familiarization tour of the western states was being made by Boeing and the airplane had been scheduled to stop at each small town along the way to promote travel by air. Fort Benton, Montana, a city of only 2,000 people, was destined to be one of these cities.

The entire town's people showed up at the pasture above the city to see the wondrous airplane. They were all amazed at how a big hulk like this, all covered with heavy metal and as big as the farmer's barn next door, ever got off the ground?

This entire event was just about the most exciting thing to have ever happened to John. He was a small child of seven at the time and an enthusiastic second grader.

Watching the first take off of that huge machine was an exciting time for the entire crowed that had gathered at the makeshift airport on the hill above the city. It was particularly exciting for John and he never forgot that special occasion so many years ago.

Interest in flying for John really didn't come about until a number of years later. Two of his brothers came home from the service shortly after the Second World War ended in 1945. One of them began taking flight training on the GI bill. Once earning his private license, he began to give friends and family rides in a brand new two place, side by side, bright and shiny Luscomb Silvare. This was the most exciting thing in John's entire life, and he was first in line every day on the flight line.

Some of the more exciting flight experiences seemed to happen when John first began to fly. This dated back many years and a quantum leap in technology had taken place within general aviation since that time.

Quite often John's brother would let him handle the controls while the airplane was in the air. This was a real thrill and provided a real sense of accomplishment to this 13 year old kid. Due to his young age, a car couldn't be legally driven, but an airplane could be flown!

Fort Benton, Montana, was a farming community, and it was customary that all the younger kids in town worked on the farms while all the older boys were in the service during the war. The only manpower available for the farms was kid power. John's early driving experience was on a McCormick Daring 15-30 iron lug wheel tractor. He was 11 years old and was so little the farmer he worked for had to crank the tractor. Then John would drive it round and round the field all day cultivating the ground.

Working on the farm seemed to be the longest single stretch of time in any young person's life, but it had provided income for John and money to do what he really wanted most, and that was to pay for flying lessons so that he could get proficient enough to fly an airplane by himself. Every cent he earned was put into a bank account, and his parents were admonished not to permit any withdraws until it was time to take flying lessons.

A number of years working on the farm had allowed John to put away enough money to join a flying club and begin flight training. The club had 20 members and owned a nearly new Aeronca Champion. The instructor was an ex-Marine major, fresh out of the US Marine Air Corps and tough as nails.

After four preliminary flight hours of instruction, John's instructor found he had mastered flight of the airplane well enough to fly it by himself. The much awaited solo flight was at hand. Upon landing, the instructor got out of the airplane and told John to make three circuits.

John suddenly found himself one thousand feet in the air and all alone at the controls. This was Christmas Day 1946 and John was 14 years old at the time. What a Christmas present this was! It was the most exciting and most pleasurable event of his entire life!

John made three circuits and three almost perfect landings. The first attempt bounced the airplane back into the air a little and he had to land it again. The second was much better and this time the airplane stayed on the ground when he landed. The final one was perfect.

John taxied over to the hanger, shut off the engine and climbed out of the airplane. He was shaking from head to toe with excitement. It took several hours for the smile to leave his face. He had accomplished something he had wanted to do every since he saw his first airplane. Now he could fly the airplane by himself.

John worked hard and earned his Private Pilots License a few months later. This new pilot was still only fifteen years old and had to pretend to be 16 in order to take the flight test. Even in those days there were rules.

Being in a small farming community sometimes had its advantages however. Somehow this particular rule was overlooked and John was given a brand new Private Pilots Certificate one full year before he was actually legal to receive one.

One of the plaguing things associated with the early days of John's flight training in the 1940's seemed to happen to some student pilots more than it did to other fellow students. The tail wheel spring of the Aeronca Champion would come loose and drop off the airplane, especially when a hard landing had been made. This occurred several times during John's early flight training.

Most instructors, particularly those who had flown from aircraft carriers while in the service of their country, were intent on having the airplane land directly on the threshold of the landing field. John's instructor was no exception. Overshooting beyond the numbers was a no no. Most students were eager to please their instructor and do this, but quite often the airplane wasn't. Characteristically most approaches were too high and too fast, and the airplane had a tendency to overshoot the intended touchdown area considerably.

John's principal instructor, being an ex-Marine fighter pilot, had landed and taken off from extremely short aircraft carriers. He was strongly influenced by his experience and this was reflected in his teaching methods. Landings were felt to be critical, particularly three point landings right on the threshold of the runway.

Often John's landing approach was a little too high. He would then attempt to stall the airplane while it was too high and the airspeed was too great. This made touching down at the right place on the threshold nearly impossible and he would overshoot.

In order to keep the instructor happy, when John was about to overshoot, he tended to pull the stick back abruptly and cause the airplane to stall. This had a near disastrous effect. With too much forward airspeed and being too high, the airplane would balloon slightly, stall, and drop to the ground hard on all three wheels. The landings would be three point landings, but the instructor wasn't too impressed by most of them. The airplane would often hit the ground near the desired touch down spot, but would drop considerably harder than it should have. The resultant bounce had knocked the spring off the tail wheel several times, and John would find himself walking out to the threshold of the runway to pick it up and carry it back to the airplane. Gradually his landing technique improved and he no longer had to face the embarrassment of knocked the spring off.

The cost of instruction in those days was $10 per hour. This included the instructor, fuel, and rental of the airplane. It is noticeably different today. The rental of a Piper Cherokee Arrow, John's current airplane at the time of this writing was typically $100 per hour, plus $35 for the instructor.

Times have changed incredibly during the past half century. The original airplane John had soloed in had three instruments, no lights, no starter, had a 65-horsepower engine, carried two people, and had a top cruising speed of 85 MPH.

John's current Piper Cherokee Arrow, has 24 flight instruments, 21 circuit breakers, three electrical systems, a starter, three radios, four navigation systems, including three navigational aid radios, and a satellite navigation system with pinpoint accuracy for navigating anywhere in the world. The push of one button will allow the airplane to fly itself to any series of way points programmed into it, hands off the controls. It has a 200 horsepower engine, seats four people, and cruises at 160 MPH, but the flying of this is getting ahead of the story.

AERONCA CHAMPION—JOHN'S FIRST AIRPLANE
TRAINER

CURRENT AIRPLANE – NOTICE THAT IT HAS A FEW MORE
GAUGES

SEVERE WIND STORM LANDING BY A NOVICE PILOT

John had one of his most unusual and exceptionally exciting experiences with only four flying hours of solo time recorded in his logbook. The year was 1948, so many years ago.

John had been taking flying lessons and had soloed with an exceptionally small amount of dual time. His ex-marine flight instructor saw in John an exceptional aptitude toward handling light aircraft. Even though he recognized John was young, he had demonstrated the confidence of a much older person and was allowed to solo with few instruction hours.

John had been flying by himself during the next few days after his exciting first solo flight. One day he arose early in the morning thinking that today was going to be another exciting solo flight in the Aeronca. Disappointment could be seen all over his face at the breakfast table as he realized the strong wind had come up and would perhaps keep him from flying that day.

He sat inside the house listening to the radio and sticking his head outside the front door every few minutes to see if the wind had died down a little. No luck was seen in the morning. He was anxious to see the weather improve so that he could jump on his bicycle and ride to the airport.

A few hours later, around 2:00 o'clock in the afternoon, the wind died down completely. It was just gone. Not a breath of air was moving. John felt this was the time to go flying! What a mistake that turned out to be!

John jumped on his bicycle and hurriedly peddled to the airport. Since there was no one else at the airport to help him start the airplane by propping it for him while he sat at the controls, he had to do it himself. He set the parking break of the Aeronca, cracked the throttle and pushed in the primer to prime the engine. Then he got out and placed a rock in front of the right wheel. He then hand propped the airplane. It started the second time over with a single loud backfire and than began to run. He hurriedly removed the rock from the front wheel, jumped in and taxied the airplane out onto the main grass runway, gunned the engine and lifted off into the smooth air.

As he was leveling off at 500 feet above the ground the airplane began to bounce all over the sky. John suddenly became aware that a terrible mistake had been made! The dead calm had been the eye of the storm and the wind began to blow hard in the opposite direction. The turbulence had caused the airplane to bounce all over the sky and had become nearly impossible for him to control. He was in serious trouble.

John attempted to keep the airplane straight and level but this became nearly impossible. He expedited his return to the airport as fast as he could get back there to land. His only option was to get the airplane down onto the ground immediately! The first difficulty was getting the airplane back to the airport at all. This became a tough job!

John's training had not progressed through crosswind landing. He had never even attempted a crosswind landing before and a landing in a storm like this was way beyond his proficiency and nearly out of the question.

John fought the controls to head the airplane toward the main runway. He entered the traffic pattern in an attempt to get to the threshold of the runway as soon as the airplane would get there.

John made a left hand turn to final and headed straight for the runway. The wind blew him drastically off alignment toward his intended touchdown point. The airplane was bouncing all over the ski as he quickly fire walled the throttle and immediately aborted his first attempt to land.

Bouncing up and down nearly completely out of control, John attempted to enter the traffic pattern again for another try on the cross runway. After fighting the strong wind to point the airplane at the second runway, he was again blown off alignment and had to abort that attempt too. This was not the runway to land on either!

Sever turbulence was bouncing the airplane in all directions. John was having tremendous difficulty just trying to find the direction the wind was coming from. He was having an even more difficult time trying to keep the airplane somewhat level under him. The wind seemed to be blowing from one direction, and then a minute later it seemed to be coming from another.

Sweat broke out on John's forehead and his entire body became as tense as a tightly drawn steel cable. He fought the controls to keep the airplane upright as he strained to find the correct runway to land on. Actually, the strong and gusty wind was blowing across the airport so that neither of the two runways was suitable for a landing.

Extreme difficulty was being experienced just keeping the airplane right side up in this ferocious wind. John found it impossible to relax even for a second from the concentration necessary to keep the airplane somewhat under control.

John circled several times as he tried to study the windsock. This was standing straight out and whipping back and forth from side to side. He tried to determine were it would be possible to land directly into the wind. There was no runway in the general direction the wind sock was pointing.

John determined that a landing would have to be made on the grass, crosswise to both the runways. By this time sweat was pouring down his forehead, running into his eyes and his hands were shaking so badly he could hardily hold onto the joystick.

John was having second thoughts about possibly landing the airplane in one piece. He was determined to try as hard as he could to keep from crashing and damaging the airplane. He knew that confidence by his instructor in his flying ability was at stake, and he was determined to get this airplane down on the ground without destroying it. Four hours of solo time in his log book was no help at all.

John picked out a spot on the grass field that would allow landing as directly into the wind as he could. Forgetting about any traffic pattern, he made a long straight in approach toward the spot he had chosen.

John's instructor had just arrived at the airport and had seen the plight of his young inexperienced student pilot and realized he was in serious trouble. He rushed out to the end of the field with his car and parked it on the grass.

John saw the car as it pulled directly onto the spot he had chosen for his touch down. It was pointed directly into the wind. John read this as being directions from his instructor to land straight in front of the car. He was right. This was the direction he had chosen too so this must have been what his instructor had tried to indicate to him.

John's knuckles were white from gripping the joystick so tightly, but he was determined to get this airplane down safely.

The airplane was bouncing up and down and jerking left and right with every new wind gust. John's hands were shaking like a leaf, sweat was rolling off him and his heart was pounding in his temples. He felt the wind was so strong; the airplane might be blown upside down just as it touched the ground.

The joystick was jittering so much from the shaking of his right hand it had affected flight of the airplane when he was banking to correct his line of decent.

John aligned the airplane directly on the front of his instructor's car. He intended to fly straight over it, stall the airplane immediately and drop onto the ground just on the far side of the car. He kept the airspeed much higher than normal for fear the airplane would loose altitude too quickly and be dashed into the car.

As the airplane approached the car it was zigzagging from side to side with every wind gust. John decided his first attempt was going to have to be the only attempt made. If the landing had to be aborted and a go around became necessary, the danger of crashing seemed too great to him. In his eyes it was now or never! Everything within John's control was going to be done to get this airplane down onto the ground in one piece.

The approach was purposely kept a little high so the wind gusts would not make one of the wings drop and hit the car. John wanted to clear the car and then touch down quickly and as close to the far side of the car as possible.

Down John flew the airplane, bouncing up and down and chinking from side to side in the gusty air. As he approached nearer to the car, a sudden strong gust made the left wing drop. John's heart was in my mouth! He over controlled the stick abruptly to compensate for this which nearly made the right wing go into the car. It missed by only inches.

Quickly the airplane was beyond the car and just a few feet above the ground. John pulled back hard on the stick. The airplane lost most of its forward motion and stalled, dropping onto the ground with a bang. The extremely strong wind, and John's pressure on the breaks, brought the airplane to a rapid stop.

The wings rocked back and forth so severely John feared a gust would get under one of them and flip the airplane up side down. For a fleeting second he just knew that his flying carrier was over.

Two instructors also sitting in the car came to his rescue. As the airplane was about to touch down, both jumped out and each rushed over and grabbed hold of a wing tip. Had they not immediately done this, the airplane would most certainly have blown over.

As John taxied the airplane forward, the weight of the instructors held the wings down onto the ground. Slowly the airplane was moved toward the airport.

The wind was so powerful the left wing rose into the air and raised one of the instructors completely off his feet, as the airplane was being turned toward the hanger. His feet were lifted at least two feet off the ground. If he had let go, there was little doubt the airplane would have flipped over.

John made a gentle turn back into the wind and the left wing came back down. Fortunately the wind eased as the lee side of the hanger was reached. The two instructors were finally able to let go of the wings. John shut the engine down and the two instructors pushed the airplane into the hanger by hand.

John's great ordeal was over! His instructor gave him a sever lecture, all about taking off in weather like this, but inside he knew that John had done a masterful job of getting the airplane safely down onto the ground.

John was just fourteen years old and completely inexperienced at the time of this event. He was lucky to have landed safely and even more fortunate the two instructors were at the airport at this particular time. They had the sense to do what was necessary to get him safely back onto the ground.

Several lessons were learned during this experience, not the least of which was a completely new respect for the weather.

An unknown wise man once said, "There are old pilots and there are bold pilots, but there are no old, bold pilots." John learned to respect this ancient wisdom and for the remainder of his flying carrier never once left for a trip by air without first seriously reviewing the current and expected weather conditions. This has served him well over his long flying carrier and he paid a fair amount of attention to making crosswind landings.

SURVIVING A FIRST SOLO CROSS COUNTRY

The events surrounding John's first solo cross country were far from the usual and had the facts been made public at the time, this experience could have nipped an extensive flying carrier before it ever got off the ground. That it did not was a credit to the competency of this young pilot and perhaps his failure to tell the full story to his instructor.

The events of John's first official solo cross-country flight somehow never seemed to get a lot of publicity around the hanger. Even his chief instructor to this day does not know the facts of that particular flight, some 55 years later. Had the true facts been related to his instructor, John felt it was quite probable that many years of flying may never have occurred.

Little ground school was taught during John's initial flight training in 1947. Most trainees in those days learned little about navigation, weather, influence of the wind, etc. This training at small air fields generally came much later, if at all.

In addition to this general lacking of knowledge being dispensed, there was little to navigate with in the airplanes of that day. Dead reckoning was about all that was available, and this was used in conjunction with the one navigational instrument in the airplane, a magnetic compass. There were no DG's, VOR's, ADF's, Loran's, or GPS's. There weren't any radios, starters, lights, and few other instruments in most airplanes of this day. This all played a part in the events of John's first solo cross-country from Fort Benton to Conrad, on to Choteau and then a return flight to Fort Benton, Montana. This was a distance of 160 miles.

John's early flight training had taken place in a 1946 Aeronca Champion. This airplane was a fabric covered, aluminum framed, two-place, tail dragger. It had a tandem seating arrangement which was preferred over most two place airplanes because the pilot sat in the front seat and the passenger sat in the rear. In most other tandem aircraft, this was just the opposite. Flying from the back seat of a J3 Piper Cub for example, was difficult because of poor visibility over the long nose of the front.

Visibility sitting in the Cub was restricted by the long engine cowl. The pilot's sitting position was so far aft the cowl restricted forward vision. This was particularly bad when attempting to make a decent landing. Once beginning to flair the nose was raised so high the pilot's forward view did not include the landing strip. The last part of the touchdown had to be made by looking out the side windows.

Visibility in the Champion was considerably better than the J3 Cub. This airplane was flown from the front seat. It didn't have all that distance in front of the pilot with its long nose hiding the view.

Being small in stature would seemingly be a disadvantage for John. He didn't allow it to be so. Not yet full-grown and small by nature, this would seem to have been a disadvantage to most people. Not so to John.

When John was a student pilot he was a long way from being full grown. This didn't deter him one bit from making adjustments to his seating arrangement and flying most airplanes of that day. He simply placed a pillow on the seat under him and another one behind his back. If not for these, the rudder pedals couldn't be reached while still seeing over the instrument panel in most airplanes.

Early flight training had progressed well for John in spite of his young years and small stature. He had soloed with just a few hours with his instructor, had flown quite a few hours and had achieved a flying proficiency belying his young age. His instructor considered him quite capable and ready for his first solo cross-country flight.

Just prior to flying his first solo however, the Flying Club sold the Aeronca John had been flying and purchased a new Luscombe Silvaire directly from the factory. The greatly anticipated first solo cross-country had to be postponed. In order to save dollars, the Flying Club had removed the engine from the Aeronca Champion and had sent it to the Luscombe factory. Here it was installed in a brand new Luscombe Silvaire.

The Luscombe was one of the first all metal general aviation airplanes. This particular one sold to the Flying Club was a two-place airplane with side by side seating. The engine removed from the Champion and installed in the Luscombe was a 65-horsepower Lycoming. Not much power compared to today's airplanes, however it preformed well in the Luscombe.

General aircraft of that day didn't have a lot of power. This same engine installed in an all aluminum, streamlined airplane like the new Luscombe would push it along at 105 MPH. This was fast for a small airplane of its time and it was highly maneuverable. In the new Luscombe, this same engine would allow the airplane to cruise 20 to 25 MPH faster than it had when installed in the original airplane it came in. Streamlining, along with light aluminum skins, had done a lot to improve the airspeed and maneuverability of all airplanes of those early years.

After the airplane was delivered, all Flying Club students were checked out in this shiny new aircraft by their instructor. At first John had difficulty learning how to fly with the joystick in his left hand instead of in his right, as it had been in the previous airplane. The Aeronca had been flown with the right hand on the stick and the left-hand on the throttle. The Luscombe had the throttle in the middle of the dashboard so the opposite was required. This was a real transition for John, and it took several flights before he become comfortable flying with his left hand.

At first John had a tendency to over control the airplane. Flying without inputting too much control on the stick had become a real chore. Once this tendency had been overcome, flying with his left hand became more natural and John learned quickly to handle the airplane smoothly with this hand. Flying with the left hand seemed to have a lighter and more delicate touch. Control of the airplane eventually became better than ever.

The maneuverability and extra speed of the new Luscombe became a real joy. The side by side seating had also become much more pleasant and visibility out the front was significantly improved. After becoming accustomed to flying the new Luscombe for several hours, the big day for John's solo cross-country flight had finally arrived. Little sleep was had the night before from the excitement of it all. John's anxiety level was very high the next morning and he was anxious to get started and to make a good showing for his instructor. This factor was all important to John as he recognized he was much younger than all the rest of the students and he was determined to make a good showing. The excitement of it all and these thoughts were going through John's head as he road his bicycle to the airport.

The first leg of the cross-country trip was to be from Fort Benton to Conrad, Montana. The next was to be from Conrad to Choteau, and the third was to return to Fort Benton, completing a triangle of just over 160 miles.

John had made the flight to Conrad and back a number of times previously with his brother, but this time it was more important. This was the big cross country solo for full credit. An all out 100 percent effort was about to be made as John prepared to prove to his instructor that a competent pilot was at the controls who had completely mastered this aircraft. He might be young, but he was determined to show his instructor just how well he could fly. He was just 15 years old.

John's instructor just might not have been so impressed if he had discovered what really happened during this flight. It is doubtful that he would have thought too much of the flying ability of this young, under age pilot, if he had really learned the truth.

Without realizing it, when preplanning and preparing for the trip, John had calculated his compass heading for his first leg in error. This error had been further compounded by a stiff side wind breeze from the direction not calculated in his equation. This was about to blow the airplane considerably off track immediately and setup the entire first leg of his cross country to a near disaster. The combination of these two elements was too much for an accurate, straight-line track to John's first destination and the stage had been set for real trouble.

Eastern Montana is nearly flat, and one bush looks like any other bush. There are few trees and few other distinctive landmarks to use as guide posts. Nearly half-way, and directly in line with the first destination, were the only distinctive landmarks in the entire area. These were two hills rising out of the flat Great Plains and were called the Knees. They were within a couple miles of each other and could not be mistaken for other hills as they were the only ones for several thousand square miles of nearly flat farming land. There were also few small towns in the entire area and none was close to John's direct route of this flight.

After a smooth and uneventful take off, John pointed his airplane in the direction that he had previously calculated. The cross country flight as "Pilot in Command" was under way with John's complete confidence. Allowance had been made for the wind strength and direction to determine his track, or so John had thought.

Apparently the strength and direction of the wind was not as accurate as it should have been, and of course the heading had been in error. This created big trouble right from the start. The initial heading of the airplane was off by several degrees, and the wind was pushing the airplane to a heading even farther away from the intended direction of track. Unknowingly, the airplane was headed nearly 45 degrees in the wrong direction.

After flying for half an hour, John felt something just didn't appear to be right. The two hills called the Knees had not come into view. When looking around in every direction, they could not be seen anywhere.

John pulled the stick back and applied full power to the engine to climb to a higher elevation for a better look. This didn't help. The Knees were nowhere to be seen at any altitude. This was perplexing and a little frightening since the Knees could generally be seen for miles and these were to be used as key visual reference points. This became a major concern.

John began to review all the pre-planning effort over and over in his mind in an attempt to determine what in the world could have gone wrong. The strong wind coming from the left could be a factor but John felt this could not cause all the problem.

As the flight continued, John's concern became greater and greater with every passing mile. The allotted time for reaching his first destination had come and gone, and the area being flown over didn't appear familiar at all. What in the world was going on!

A knot had rapidly developing in the pit of John's stomach. Even though this country had been flown over a number of times before, nothing seemed familiar. There had been few clues to tell him the airplane had been heading in the wrong direction. Except for not finding the Knees hills, the area appeared the same as it always had. It was all perfectly flat farming country and nearly all featureless. What in the world had gone wrong?

The first leg of the triangle flight was to have taken 45 minutes. After flying for 45 minutes, it become all too apparent that something had gone drastically wrong, but what? Looking out the window of the airplane, nothing could be seen that appeared familiar. Conrad wasn't there and not a single other friendly landmark could be found. Even the bushes looked different. The knot in John's stomach was increasing and John's confidence had begun to slip. Sweat began to form on his forehead.

Great concern was being felt for what the instructor was going to think if the flight had to be made back to his home base without finding the first stop. Since this was John's first official solo cross-country flight, this just had to not happen. He just had to work this out without returning to his home base. His reputation was at stake and was dependent upon finding his way to the first destination.

If it becomes necessary to fly back to Fort Benton without finding Conrad, the embarrassment would be just too painful. John was determined to work this out and he had to come up with a plan of action that made some sense and that could correct this mistake. He felt he must do this and he had to do it now.

Turning to the left and flying west, John reasoned, would bring the airplane to a major highway. There was only one major highway in this area going North and South and John felt he must find it. This was the only prominent feature other than the Knees, but flying to this would have been a bit out of the way.

After intersecting the highway, the problem would then be which way to turn in order to fly on to Conrad. Had he flown the airplane too far north and would come out beyond Conrad, or would he come out too far south and arrive at the highway before Conrad? Should he then have to turn to the right or to the left? This problem was put aside and would have to be dealt with later, after the highway had been found.

John turned the airplane 90 degrees to the west and continued the flight for another 15 minutes. Conrad didn't show up and neither did the highway!

John could see a line of trees about ten miles away. Perhaps this was a small town. If the name of the town could be determined, this might allow him to gain his bearings. Perhaps he could make a low pass over this to determine what town it was. Often the name of the town was written on the water tower or some other prominent building.

John turned the airplane 30 degrees to the north and flew for another 5 minutes before reaching the trees. This turned into a major disappointment. The trees turned out to be a windbreak surrounding a farmhouse and not a town at all. Another hope had died which placed another large lump in John's throat. He turned the airplane back west again and continued onward for another 15 minutes wondering what next he should do. This was getting serious. There was still no sign of Conrad or of the major highway! What if he should fly so long that he became low on fuel? Then the worrying would really start!

By this time John's concern had turned to near fear. The highway hadn't been intersected, and Conrad wasn't anywhere to be found. This hadn't made any sense. Neither had anything else been recognized that could have been used to get out of this mess. Fear had become nearly paralyzing, but giving up was not an option. John gathered his emotions together and determined this was not going to overwhelm him. He was going to work his way out of this!

The airplane had now been in the air for 40 minutes longer than it should have been to arrive at John's first destination. His hands were beginning to shake as the flight continued for another 10 minutes. Nothing!

What in the world can be done now? By this time his hands on the stick and throttle were beyond a little sweaty and the shaking had started in earnest. A disturbing feeling was developing in the pit of his stomach.

John's mind went into a whirlwind. If he turned back, how would he ever find his home airport? Obviously the flight had gone the wrong direction. Several turns had been made attempting to locate something familiar. After all of this maneuvering and misdirection, if the airplane was turned around, and an attempt was made to fly back to Fort Benton, the problem would only be compounded. The direction to fly back was as much a mystery as the direction to fly onward. Sweat began to pour off John's forehead, and the realization of possibly being lost was becoming very real.

John continued his flight for several more minutes while trying to decide what to do. A landing could be attempted in some farmer's yard if he began to be low on fuel, but that seemed risky. The airplane could be damaged by a bad landing on unfamiliar ground. There could easily be a ditch or a guy wire or something that could not be seen until it was too late. This didn't seem to be a very good option. Besides, it would be embarrassing to land and have to say to some farmer, "Where am I?" John's best bet seemed to be to continue on and attempt to find something familiar. Fortunately fuel was not too low—at this stage.

The best approach seemed to still be to attempt to find the highway. If the flight was to continue long enough to the west, the airplane would eventually have to come to it. Once this could be found, John reasoned, the airplane could be turned north. Even though it would not be known whether Conrad was to the north or to the south, this would give him another out. By finding the highway and turning north, John would eventually come to the Marias River. This would be a prominent feature and could lead to a way out. If need be, the river could be followed to the Missouri River and from there it would be an easy matter to find the way back to John's home base. This would be a long way out of the way, but at least it would get the airplane back home—providing the fuel didn't run out!

This idea wasn't exciting to John though, because the instructor would have to be told that he had failed to fly a good solo cross-country. This was serious business for a young pilot on his first solo cross-country. John's major concern was still what kind of impression this flight was going to make on his instructor.

Suddenly another larger line of trees was spotted in the distance. John turned the airplane toward these and flew for another ten minutes. There appeared to be a lot more trees than the first bunch. Perhaps this was a small town! Maybe a pass could be made low enough to be able to read the name of the town on the water tower.

John flew on for another 5 minutes. It was a small town! The water tower was located and the airplane was dived low enough to read the writing on the side of the tank. It said C-O-N-R-A-D. Wow! It was Conrad! The town that had been lost for so long!

A 45-minute flight had turned into a 95-minute flight or 50 minutes off course in 45 minutes. A 65-mile trip had turned into a 135-mile long, tense and terrifying ordeal.

The airport was quickly located and a landing was hurriedly made. The operator of the field signed John's logbook to indicate to the instructor that the airplane had been flown there. The operator was somehow not advised what had just happened. This fact was history and was going to remain so, at least for the time being.

While the airplane was being fueled, all the navigation data for the next two legs of the trip was re-figured. This wasn't going to happen again! The remainder of the trip was flown without further incident.

This entire episode was so embarrassing that somehow the true facts were not related to anyone for many years. To this day, even though John has kept in contact with his original instructor, these facts were never brought out to him. Somehow all the requirements for a private license had been fulfilled, including this solo cross-country flight. John did, however, neglect to tell the instructor that he was only fifteen years old when the final flight test had taken place for his private license. (Regulations require the applicant be sixteen years of age in order to qualify for a private license.) Somehow this was never made an issue and John received his private license that summer, a few months before his sixteenth birthday.

Shortly after this flight, and perhaps as a result of it, much more seriousness had been attached to ground school and particularly to navigational training. This had been a good lesson, and never again would it take as long for John to find an airport as it did to fly to this one. Modern day equipment such as GPS (satellite navigation system) certainly had made this job a lot easier.

THAT'S NO WAY TO BUY AN AIRPLANE

Some times an account of just what not to do in an airplane comes to light. A classic example of this occurred many years ago in a small country town in the state of Montana. Because of the bazaar nature of this incident, it may seem not to be factual; however this story is based on a true incident and is an account of an actual occurrence.

During the late 1940's, two of John's uncles bought a two place, side-by-side seating, all fabric Taylorcraft airplane. This was a good general aviation aircraft for its day.

All their lives these two brothers had driven heavy machinery. Each had his own road building outfit and was more than familiar with almost every known piece of road building equipment available. They were both in their early 30's at the time and perhaps, to hear them tell it, knew more about heavy machinery than most people knew about their own automobiles. Nearly every piece of heavy equipment in existence had been owned and driven by them at one time or another.

Without ever having flown an airplane, or having taken a single lesson, they went out to the airport and bought this airplane. Since no trouble had been experienced handling any other piece of machinery, they figured this little airplane could certainly not be a problem. After all, much bigger and more complicated equipment had been driven than this, and after all, it was just another piece of machinery and a small one at that.

The two brothers answered an ad in the local newspaper for a "nearly new, flown few hours, in perfect condition, Taylorcraft".

They drove out to the local airport and had a look at this magnificent Taylorcraft flying machine. Even though there was a little of the fabric covering hanging down from the fuselage, one bent wheel strut and a missing propeller nose cone, the two expert equipment operators were impressed with the little airplane. It had a reasonably poor paint job, but that was easy enough to fix. The engine seemed to run good, even though it coughed a little and obviously needed a good tune-up and a little of the oil cleaned off the outside.

The owner demonstrated the airplane by flying each prospective buyer around the landing pattern, making somewhat of a reasonable landing each time. By now, each uncle was really excited about owning and flying this airplane. A decision was made on the spot to buy it and to take immediate delivery.

Their checkbooks were taken out of their shirt pockets, their money was put down, they climbed into the airplane, somehow managed to get it started, and took off into the air, leaving the previous owner standing with his mouth open.

Once in the air, to hear them describe it, the airplane was all over the sky. They both became a little concerned at this time and decided they had better get this bucking bronco back down onto the ground. Neither of them had the slightest idea how to fly an airplane, let alone how to land one.

They managed to turn the airplane OK, even though the turns were rough enough to throw them up onto the side of the cabin as nearly violent skidding turns were executed to the left and then to the right. After flying around for quite some time trying to figure out how to handle this maverick, they somehow managed to find the airport and arrive near the landing end of it. Little did they know they had actually found the wrong airport. The next task was to try to get this airplane onto the ground without killing themselves.

The first attempt was a complete disaster! Without cutting power, the airplane was pointed at the ground and an attempt to bring it down somewhere near the closest end of the runway was made. As this was done, the airplane picked up speed, traveled much too far along the runway, and swooped up as they quickly came to the opposite end of the landing strip. Instantly, it was decided they had better not try to land this time after all. This was all going to be a little harder than they had figured!

During the next go around, they decided they would somehow slow the airplane down a little so the runway wouldn't go by so fast and wouldn't be overrun as they were about to touch down. As the threshold of the runway was approached, power was cut back about half way. Their eyeballs became decidedly larger as they hit the ground with a tremendous bang and bounced back into the air. Fortunately they slammed on full power as this happened. The airplane remained in one piece and was still flying even though the bounce into the air was spectacular.

By this time a small crowed of spectators had gathered to watch the strange activity going on. It was readily apparent to them that whoever was flying that airplane, or trying to, was really in trouble.

After the two attempts, these two would be pilots quickly came to the conclusion this was not going to work. They were going to have to figure something else out in order to get this beast back down onto the ground.

On the next attempt they planned to cut the power back even farther, and slow the airplane down even more, just before approaching the landing strip.

The airplane was lined up on the field from a long way out and the power was reduced. The airplane began to descend too fast. They were about to hit the fence between them and the threshold when power was frantically applied back on. Back into the air they went to try something else, since obviously that wasn't the answer either.

Little by little, a light crosswind began to increase. On the next attempt the airplane was pushed off to the side and couldn't be lined up with the runway. Around they went again. Next time they would start over on the upwind side a little farther.

Three more passes were made at the ground. Fortunately the crosswind abated a little and they at least were not pushed sideways off the runway. Each time the airplane came close to the ground; however, it would buck up and down so much they would hit full power and climb back into the air again. They were always coming out too short or too long.

Finally on the eighth try, they decided the airplane would have to be slowed down as much as possible, just before reaching the runway. As the runway was approached, power was cut back completely. Unfortunately, they didn't have a clue how to use the carburetor heat, so this was not activated. This time the threshold of the runway was reached before nearly touching down. Ground effect made them float to the center of the landing strip where they were about to stall and touch the ground. The opposite end of the runway was coming up very fast. Suddenly the engine quit! The silence was absolutely deafening! They were committed to land whether they wanted to or not.

All four feet were nearly forced through the firewall as both "pilot and co-pilot" were putting the brakes on while still in the air. As the airplane came closer to the ground, they pulled the nose up, and in so doing, lost all of their forward speed and the airplane stalled. The airplane was still about ten feet in the air.

The airplane literally fell out of the sky and hit the ground with a tremendous thud, bouncing about 20 feet into the air. The first bounce nearly drove the landing gear through the bottom of the airplane. The second bounce created a very loud bang and the airplane bounced back into the air once again. When the airplane quite bouncing and began to roll somewhat sideways down the field, it ran off the end of the runway, through a fence and ended up about a hundred yards into a cow pasture. Fortunately, the fence at the far end of the landing strip was not very strong. It gave way without significant damage to the airplane or its occupants, other then ripping most of the fabric off the understructure of the airplane. They were down on the ground and they were still alive!

Both brothers were shaken so badly it took several minutes for them to even crawl out of the airplane. By the time the airplane came to a stop, the small crowd that had gathered to witness all the excitement had ran down to the airplane and helped them to get out.

The landing had been made at an airport several miles from the one they had taken off from. Obviously in shock from their ordeal, they were even more confused when this was found out. In all of their excitement, they weren't even aware they had made this miraculous landing at a different airport from the one they had taken off from.

These two, by now, flight experienced brothers, climbed out of the airplane, sat down on the ground and just sat there for a few minutes trying to gain their composure. When finally regaining strength in their leg muscles, they got up and walked over to the nearest country road and hitchhiked back to their home airport.

Finally upon arriving at their home airport, they promptly walked into the office and signed up for a few flying lessons!

Ironically, both brothers ended up flying light aircraft for more than 50 years, and both currently own their own airplan.

FLIGHT SCHOOL– LONG ISLAND, NEW YORK

After many years working as an Industrial Engineer for the Boeing Company, John went on a two year assignment for the Company to New York. His responsibility was as Manufacturing Surveillance to Fairchild Republic at their two facilities, one in Farmingdale, New York, and the other in Hagerstown, Maryland. Both factories were located on large airports which gave John the opportunity to log some time in a variety of airplanes.

Originally, the main factory in Farmingdale, Long Island, New York was the huge Republic Aircraft Company. This company had designed and manufactured the P47 fighter during the Second World War and later designed and built the F105 jet fighter flown in Korea and Vietnam.

The other factory located in Hagerstown, Maryland was the original Fairchild factory. The much smaller Fairchild Company had just bought out the much larger Republic Aircraft Company. The mouse had just swallowed the cat.

The Fairchild Aircraft Company had designed and manufactured many of the early airplanes dating back to the 20's and 30's. Much later, after the Vietnam War, they designed and manufactured numerous helicopters as well as the twinjet ground support fighter, referred to as the Warthog, the US Air Force A10. This airplane had a huge gattling gun, which was as long as a Volkswagen and weighed two-ton. It fired 6,000 rounds per minute and was used extensively in the Gulf War as a tank buster, as well as for other ground support operations.

While on the assignment at Fairchild Republic, John attended flight school for the second time. Flying had changed a great deal since the early days and it did not pay to be out of touch. The plan was to buy an airplane upon retirement and it was necessary to be prepared to use it properly. Retirement was not to be too many years in the future.

Seven weeks of ground school and another seven weeks of instrument training were taken, along with advanced flight training. Nearly every evening during the summer was spent in the air. The data studied and learned was significantly more than it was the first time around and flying in the busy New York area was invaluable experience.

One of the first things learned was to try to keep the number of landings equal to the number of takeoffs. The next thing learned was that if you pushed the stick forward, the houses get bigger. If you pull the stick back, they get smaller – unless you keep pulling the stick back—then they get bigger again.

The flights from Republic Field were interesting since this was one of the more busy airports on Long Island. On one particularly busy Saturday afternoon flight, there were four airplanes flying in the traffic pattern in front and three more behind John. His down wind leg was extended by the control tower until the airport could not even be seen. On final, the Cessna 152 flown that day was so slow one airplane had to pass John in order to stay in the traffic pattern.

Charles Lindbergh had flown over much of this same area on his famous nonstop trip to Paris. He started from Roosevelt Field, which is now a horse race track and a shopping center. His flight was over Long Island Sound, Newport, Rhode Island, over Cape Cod and on out over the ocean. This same route was flown by John a number of times. Each time he would imagine what it must have been like to leave land and not expect to see it again for many hours, especially in an airplane the vintage of the Spirit of St. Louis.

One of the more eventful trips John made in a small airplane while there was from Farmingdale, Long Island, to Hagerstown,

Maryland. Another Boeing manager was visiting the Fairchild facilities and went with him. A four place Piper 180 was rented and flown to Hagerstown for a two-day visit and then a quick return to Farmingdale was made for further meetings.

Commercial flights from New York to Hagerstown were cumbersome at best. A commercial trip required a drive to Kennedy Airport, a flight to Baltimore, where a change of airplanes was required, and then an onward flight to Hagerstown. Traveling required a 1 hour drive to the airport, turn in of the rental car, a wait in the airline-waiting lounge, a second wait in the airline lounge between planes, and then a second flight from Baltimore to Hagerstown.

Traveling this way would take all day and pretty much exhaust the travelers in the process. Rather than flying commercially, a trip was planned in a Piper Cherokee 180 rented at Republic Field. The aerial distance between Farmingdale and Hagerstown was 200 nautical miles and would take only 1-1/2 hours to fly there in this airplane. This was considerably faster than flying commercially

From the factory to the parking area in front of the Republic Field Flight Center was a five-minute drive. The car was left there. From the parking area to the airplane was a walk of twenty feet to the airplane. Both climbed into the airplane, strapped themselves in and were on their way with little effort and very little delay of time.

The route of flight was to be very interesting and scenic. They would fly directly over Manhattan Island, over down town New York City, across Newark, New Jersey, on into Pennsylvania, and beyond into the northern part of Maryland.

In order to fly over New York City with its three airports, Kennedy, La Guardia, and Newark, flight control required all small aircraft to fly above 7,000 feet. This is required because of the Terminal Control Area surrounding these three airports. It is not advisable to be interfering with the much faster jet traffic. From Republic Field in Farmingdale, the Terminal Control Area begins immediately and extends sixty miles to the west, directly on the route of flight to Hagerstown.

After takeoff, it was necessary to circle several times in order to climb from sea level to 8,500 feet before starting toward their destination.

Even though the airplane was quite high, jet traffic could be seen landing directly under them at Kennedy Airport as they flew over that area. From there the flight went over Brooklyn and over the East River, which separated Long Island from Manhattan Island. The buildings of the New York skyline were seen directly in front of the airplane. The United Nations Building, the Chrysler Building, the Pan American Building, the Empire State Building and the two World Trade Center Buildings were prominently displayed.

John made a slow steep turn directly over the Empire State Building. Two complete circles were made and the view straight down the face of the building, all the way to the ground, was spectacular. Although small, cars on the streets and people on the sidewalks could be seen.

Manhattan Island is quite long, but is fairly narrow. It took only three or four minutes to cross the major New York City area before coming to the Hudson River. This separates New York City's downtown area on Manhattan Island from the mainland.

Once above the city the route of flight changed to the southwest so that Ellis Island could be flown over. This island appeared to be just large enough to house the immigration building. Little land could be seen, except directly under the massive former immigration building

From this location, the Statue of Liberty was directly in front of the aircraft. John made another slow steep turn over this and the lady holding her torch seemed close to them and impressive. The airplane was now more than a mile above the people on the ground. They could be seen but were quite tiny.

John continued their flight over New Jersey. After a few minutes the Control Area was flown out of and it was possible to drop down to a lower altitude where the view of the countryside was much better. In short order the Delaware River came into view and was crossed into Pennsylvania. The next point of interest was the Civil War Battlefield at Gettysburg.

John circled the battlefield several times. The cannons of both the Northern and Southern armies were plainly visible. The battlefield area was much larger than previously realized. On one side of the battlefield was the memorial stand where Abraham Lincoln gave his Gettysburg Address. Altitude of the airplane was held at 1500 feet above the ground and was so close to the memorial stand that it was easy to imagine the words, "Four score and seven years...". The actual platform of the gazebo where Lincoln stood while giving his address could plainly be seen. It was an awesome sight.

At one end of the massive battlefield could be seen Dwight and Mamie Eisenhower's farm. The main building appeares to be a large southern style mansion. John decided not to fly directly over the mansion where the people might be disturbed. Then too, a surface to air missile sent after them just might not be too comforting. He flew several hundred feet to one side of the buildings, but was close enough to be able to see seven limousines parked in the circular driveway. The Eisenhower's must have been entertaining dignitaries.

It was only a short distance from the Eisenhower's farm to the Pennsylvania/Maryland border and on to Hagerstown. The total flight took less than two hours, even with all the sightseeing. This same trip by flying the commercial airlines would have taken seven hours.

Hagerstown was known to have an outstanding seafood restaurant. John would visit this whenever the opportunity arose. Specialty of the house was whole crabs cooked in their shells. A few preliminary courses were necessary before getting to the crabs.

Several different types of seafood were on the Ala Carte menu. The starter was generally Maryland crab cakes. No one in the world can make crab cakes like those served in this restaurant. A pitcher of beer was always in order. The next course chosen was shrimp stuffed with crabmeat. Then came raw clams, raw oysters, fried oysters that melted in their mouths, soft-shelled crabs, and Chesapeake Bay shrimp.

About this time John and his business associate's stomachs were about to burst. The waiter then removed everything from the table, including the tablecloth, covered the table with a piece of butcher paper, and dumped a bucket of crabs onto the table.

The crabs were cooked in a spicy sauce, and except for being cleaned, were still in their shells. A one-inch square wooden "crab knocker" was provided to each of them for cracking the crabs. Even though they were both nearly filled to capacity, the crabs were so delicious; the entire bucket full seemed to disappear in very short order. What a tremendous meal this was. Breakfast the next day had to be a little on the lean side.

Business was completed early the next morning and the airplane was flown back to Republic Field in Farmingdale, Long Island. This required another short 2 hour flight as compared to a 7 hour commercial flight ordeal.

FLYING ADVENTURES IN FIJI

In 1973, John accepted an assignment as Boeing's Manufacturing Surveillance Manager to the Australian Aircraft Industry. This became the first of two assignments of four years each to Australia.

The first trip to Melbourne was exciting and memorable. It was very, very long. The flight took 24 hours from the time John and his wife Carol left the ground in Seattle until the airplane landed in Melbourne.

The first leg of the trip was from Seattle to Los Angeles and then on to Honolulu. The airplane flown was one of the early 707's. The airline had two movies on board, which helped to pass the first nine hours. The Mai Tai in the waiting room of the Honolulu Airport seemed to help a bit also during the two-hour layover for the next airplane to Fiji.

It was quite warm in Honolulu and there was only time for one refreshing drink. It turned out to be a bigger one than they had anticipated. The coconut glass it came in was about the size of a fish bowl. It had fresh mint, pineapple, and a big piece of sugar cane floating in the center. The rum punch was tasty and refreshing and helped John and Carol a great deal to recover from their first nine hours of the marathon flight.

A mini vacation was planned to break up the long travel time from Seattle to Melbourne by stopping for several days in the Fijian Islands. Planned originally as just a rest stop, this became a major vacation and was one of the most pleasant things John and Carol had ever experienced. This stop over was repeated as often as possible during many trips to and from Australia in later years.

After an extremely long third leg, John and Carol finally arrived in Nandi, Fiji more asleep than awake. It was 3:00 o'clock in the morning, local time, and they had been awake since 5:00 AM Pacific time the morning before.

Exhaustion was really settling in by the time the airplane arrived on the ground. Customs was cleared in pretty much a blur. Traveling to this point had taken more than 19 hours, and the total wakeful hours had included an additional 12 hours. No real rest was seen for 31 hours. There was still another 45 miles to go in a taxi before the inside of a hotel room could be seen. Looking forward to a glorious bed and restful sleep was becoming an agony and their eyes were beginning to close in the tropical heat and high humidity. Even at 3:00 o'clock in the morning the temperature was 80 degrees and the humidity was at least 90 %.

The "Coral Coast" of Fiji is located on the opposite side of the island from the city of Nandi. The beautiful beaches and best resorts are located here and the only way to get there is by local taxi.

The road to the Coral Coast has to be the strangest John and Carol had ever seen. One side of the road is paved while the other side is not. The roadbed, even on the paved side, is narrow and full of chuckholes.

Without realizing, or perhaps in their over tired dazed condition, they didn't notice the driver was sitting on the right hand side of the car. The taxi was driven out onto the main road which had only one side paved.

Immediately, two cars came plummeting straight toward the taxi with their bright lights shining in John's and Carol's eyes. Those idiotic drivers passed on the wrong side! After the sudden shock and realization that this had actually happened, they abruptly became aware the Fijians drive on the opposite side of the road, just like the Australians do.

The taxi driver drove along with all four wheels on the paved part of the road until an approaching car came at him on a collision course. Then, at the last possible moment, the driver swerved off to the left side in order to allow the other car to pass. Several times, to the sleepy minds of the passengers, it appeared that a collision was imminent. This tended to get John's and Carol's attention real quick, and even in their overly tired state, they suddenly became wide awake within the first few minutes of this fantastic ride. The tension was intense!

An hour and a half later the taxi finally arrived at their destination, the fabulous Fijian Resort. It was still dark when they arrived at 4:30 AM., and little could be seen of the hotel or surrounding grounds. In their exhausted state, there was little interest in sightseeing anyway. After checking in, the inside of the room and the bed was all they could think about. Having a good look around would have to wait.

After sleeping for two hours, both John and Carol were wide-awake. It was still only 6:00 AM in Fiji and the sun was just come up. The time difference between Fiji and Seattle was four hours. By six o'clock in the morning in Fiji, it is already ten o'clock in Seattle. This was well past John's and Carol's normal get up time and neither of them was able to go back to sleep, even as tired as they were.

Carol pulled the curtain back on the sliding glass window to have a look. They both took a peek outside and both let out a gasp. The view nearly took their breath away. Their eyes could hardly believe the fantastic tropical view directly in front of them, it was so magnificent! Both thought this place had to be one of the most beautiful places in the world.

The view was over a grassy area, surrounded by palm trees and lush tropical flowers, to a lovely glistening white sand beach, with a bright blue, gently rolling surf washing onto the shore. What a picture made in heaven!

The hotel complex is located on a small island about 500 yards from the mainland. The water is the most beautiful blue imaginable, which contrasts vividly with the extremely white sand and the green of the tropical vegetation. Beautiful Bougainvillea and other tropical flowers are everywhere. Across the water, the mainland could be seen with the magnificent green foliage and brightly colored tropical flowers. Palm trees, green grass, red flowers, white sand, and blue ocean was visible as far as the eye could see. It just took their breath away, it was so beautiful.

Breakfast was served in the main open-air dinning room that first morning. This dinning area is located on a small hill overlooking the sandy beach and ocean. The view from there is over the tropical garden, with its brightly colored flowers, palm trees and other tropical vegetation, to the coral reef where the larger ocean waves were breaking. There are six other restaurants in this magnificent resort paradise.

The island the resort is built on is located on a beautiful bay. The entrance from the ocean is protected by a large coral reef across the opening to the bay. The larger ocean waves are broken by this coral reef and are kept from hitting the shore of the island with much force. Gentle surf reaches the island inside the bay and is almost mesmerizing to watch as it effortlessly flows onto the glistening white sandy beach.

The water is quite warm for swimming. It is consistently above 80 degrees. The depth of the water is only 10 to 20 feet deep for nearly 100 feet away from the shore. It can't be any nicer for swimming and snorkeling in this tropical paradise.

John and Carol rented flippers, facemasks, and snorkels and swimming was the order for part of the day, every day for the rest of that week.

Breakfast was always in the open air restaurant overlooking the fantastic tropical setting and the magnificent white sandy beach and bright blue gentile surf.

Most of their days were spent in the water which never seemed to get cold. The coral on the shallow bottom is a multitude of shades of green, blue, pink, red, orange, and white; every color imaginable. Hundreds of tropical fish in various sizes are everywhere. John and Carol spent so much time snorkeling to view the intricate coral and the tropical fish that their backs were exposed to the sun long enough to became a bit sunburned. Other than this miner problem, the island could easily have become home for the rest of eternity.

Returning to reality was a struggle when several days later John and Carol had to depart for the airport.

Just prior to leaving Seattle, one of the executive managers of Hawker de Havailland (HDH) had provided a telephone number for

John to call to arrange a tour by airplane around Fiji. The Air Pacific airline in Fiji was owned and operated by a subsidiary of HDH.

The day before John and Carol were due to leave, John called the airline and the message from HDH management was relayed. The airline graciously arranged a flight around the main island of the Fijian chain in a twin-engine Beechcraft. This was to be flown by a captain from Air Pacific Airlines. In order to get to the landing area for pickup, John's instructions were to take a taxi from the resort hotel to a pasture located on the mainland several miles away. This was the only area close by which was large enough to facilitate the landing and taking off of an airplane as large as the twin engine Beechcraft.

On the way to the airfield in a rickety old taxi, the left rear brake began to drag and make a terrible racket. It appeared the taxi driver was going to stop and leave John and Carol stranded in the middle of nowhere. If the taxi driver would have stopped to repair it, they would have missed their connection and the ride in the airplane would have been off. This was serious!

Even though it was nearly 90 degrees, with no air conditioning in the taxi, John rolled up all the windows in the back so the terrible noise could not be heard as loudly. He then began to talk to the taxi driver in very loud tones. This distracted him somewhat and he kept on going. The ploy must have worked because he drove on a few more miles to the field where the airplane was waiting for them.

After introductions were made to the 707 Captain flying the airplane, all climbed on board and off they went into the air. That poor taxi driver was left to his own devices with a major problem on his hands. It was a good thing John had given him an extra big tip when paying the bill because it was apparent the taxi driver was going to have a big repair bill.

The flight was magnificent! The route began along the Coral Coast (southern cost) where most of the large resorts and the magnificent beaches are located. Sunbathers on the beaches could be seen and many of them waved as the airplane flew over their heads.

Several small islands were flown over and a good view of the magnificent resorts on them was plainly visible. The pilot flew low enough to allow them to see swimmers in the water off the lovely coconut palm studded beaches. What a glorious sight that was.

Back over the main island they flew. Soon they came to a large pineapple plantation. Several workers were seen in the field picking the pineapple. An extremely small landing strip was located along side the pineapple field. The pilot made a spectacular landing on this small dirt strip.

Not only was the landing strip extremely short, it pointed down hill and had a large drop off at the far end. In addition to this set of difficulties, the landing had to be made down wind.

The skill of this pilot was exceptional however; and the airplane touched down on the first few feet of the landing strip. The airplane decelerated rapidly with heavy usage of the breaks and came to a rapid stop several feet to spare. Wow! This was a big airplane for such a short field, but the pilot was up to the task and he made it look easy.

All piled out of the airplane to stretch their legs while the pilot talked to the plantation foreman. He was going to treat them to fresh pineapple, right from the vine. The foreman had one of the young men working there go out into the field and pick several fresh pineapple right from the vine. He brought them back to the airplane and trimmed them into pineapple "popsicles". Each one had a handle cut from the stem. The fruit was nice and cool and refreshing and the taste was outstanding. Since taken directly from the vine, they were the sweetest John and Carol had ever eaten. What a fabulous rest stop this was out in the remote jungle of Fiji in 90 degree tropical heat.

Back into the air they all went with plenty of room to spare for the takeoff. The pilot continued the flight along the northern coast of the main and largest island of the Fijian chain. Several other islands could be seen in the distance. Fiji consisted of more than 200 islands. With the exception of the two large main islands, the rest are quite small.

As they flew to the east end of the largest island, two rivers could be seen in the distance in the shape of an ever-widening "V". Where they met the sea they were about 30 miles apart. At the water's edge was a magnificent white sand beach stretching all the way from one river to the other. In between the long expanse of the two rivers was a bright, white sand beach, which was offset by the brilliant blue of the ocean and the lush green of the tropical jungle. It was a glorious sight. Not a single person could be seen along the entire 30-mile stretch of beach. The pilot told John and Carol this area is not inhabited because there are no bridges across the two rivers. The beach is totally inaccessible, except by sea.

The pilot went on to tell John and Carol this beach had a colorful history. Charles Kingsford Smyth, on his famous first flight across the Pacific from America to Australia, landed at Nandi, Fiji for fuel. He had flown for 35 hours after taking off from Los Angeles, landing in Hawaii, and then flying on to Fiji. There was still another 20 hours of actual flight time remaining for "Smythie" to fly in order to reach Australia.

Smythie made a landing in a large field next to a schoolhouse when he first arrived in Fiji. The field was adequate for landing but was much too short for his departure. The fuel necessary for the remaining flight from Fiji to Australia would have made the airplane so heavy he would not have had a takeoff area long enough for the airplane to get off the ground. A much longer runway was required than the little field next to the schoolhouse.

"Smythie" as he was known, solved this problem in a novel way. The wings were removed and the airplane was barged around the island to this lovely 30-mile long, completely isolated beach. This by itself was a major feat since the airplane had to be moved nearly 150 miles.

The airplane was fueled and made ready for takeoff. Smythie ran the airplane down the sandy beach between the two rivers a long way before ever wobbling tenuously into the air. Once off the ground and airspeed built up, Smythie was able to complete the first ever flight from America to Australia. The year was 1928, a few years before general aviation became popular in most countries.

The actual airplane Kingsford Smyth flew on this historic flight is a Faulker Tri Motor named the Southern Cross. It is on display near Brisbane, Queensland, in Australia.

Smythie disappeared seven years after this historic flight, while he was over the Indian Ocean attempting to make a record flight from England back to Australia.

Continuing on John and Carol's flight, the pilot pointed out a relatively small island off the east coast of the main island. This particular island was the home of the native Fijians who had conquered all of the Fijian Island chain. The pilot pointed out this island had the largest collection of human remains found anywhere in the world. These Fijians were cannibals. They ate all of their captives and left their bones to dry in the sun.

John and Carol's great air tour ended when they landed at the airport in Nandi. The airport had an unusually long 15,000 foot runway. It had been built by the Americans for landing B17's, B24's, C47's, B29's and the like during the Second World War.

John and Carol's landing was made on the far end of the extremely long runway. The airplane had to be taxied for a very, very long way to the terminal on the opposite end. The airplane could have taken off and landed three or perhaps even four times, without ever using the entire landing area.

Real VIP treatment was afforded John and Carol when they arriving at the terminal. Their bags were offloaded from the Twin Beach and loaded directly on board a Qantas 707. John and Carol, "the Boeing People", were escorted into the administration building where they were provided towels, wash cloths and bars of soap and directed to the showers. After spending all day in this tropical heat, this was a refreshing respite before climbing on board the 707 for the last leg of the trip to Australia.

It was with great reluctance that John and Carol said goodbye to this magnificent tropical paradise with its outstanding aerial tour. After the royal VIP treatment on the airplane and at the airport, it was even more difficult for them to return to reality for the last two legs of the flight to Sydney, with a second flight on to Melbourne, Australia.

FIJIAN RESORT

ACTUAL AIRPLANE KINGSFORD SMITH MADE HIS
HISTORIC FIRST FLIGHT ACROSS THE PACIFIC FROM
AMERICA TO AUSTRALIA IN 1928

CULTURAL DIFFERENCES DISCOVERED IN AUSTRALIA

John and Carol found significant differences in Australia from that experienced back home in America, particularly with the language. Unconsciously they had both assumed, "because English was the common language, everything else could be expected to be the same". This couldn't have been farther from the truth! Winston Churchill once said "America and England were linked together by an uncommon language". John and Carol found this to be true of America and Australia.

Upon arrival in Melbourne, little of the English being spoken by the Australians could even be understood. The Aussie accent seemed strong and disconcerting to John and Carol to understand what was being said. The colloquialisms used were particularly bothersome since most were totally different words. Some were similar words used to mean something entirely different from their normal usage back home. Many of the words were the same, but were found not to mean the same. Some terms were completely foreign and meaningless to the ear, such as "dinky die" and "fair dinkum".

A classic example of words used differently was the word "bushed". When bushed in America, a person is tired. This word doesn't mean the same thing in Australian. Here it means to be lost, as out in the bush (backcountry).

John and Carol began to spend many hours studying the local television programs before this "new" language became very comfortable.

Speaking of a failure to communicate, an interesting event took place during the early days of their stay in Melbourne. The location of the two factories in Melbourne doing business with Boeing had not been located yet. When out for one of their first drives around the city of Melbourne, John and Carol decided to locate these. This would be a good quest for the afternoon.

Driving around looking for these two factories became confusing. None of the streets were square and many had names rather than numbers. After a while, it became apparent little progress was being made toward finding the factories. John stopped the car and asked a policeman standing on the corner for directions to the Government Aircraft Factory. His response was, "Blimey! You blokes are really bushed! You go down past that chook lorry, go past the second set of bousers, turn left, go across on the punt and you will be in the factory area. Fair dinkum! She'll be right mate!" The only thing John and Carol understood from all of this was that a left-hand turn had to be made somewhere down the street.

Translation: Blimey! (My God). You blokes (casual acquaintances) are really bushed (lost). You go down past the chook lorry (chicken truck), go past the second set of bousers (gas pumps), go across the punt (cross the river on the ferry) and you will be in the factory area. Fair dinkum (I am telling you true). She'll be right (everything will be OK) mate (friend).

One of the first meals in Australia was even more of a disaster. In Australia an entree is not the main course, as it is in America. It is an appetizer. This led to real confusion and became a real comedy of errors between John and the waiter.

A major miscommunication occurred at one of the first restaurant they frequented. It was spectacular! The waiter asked what John wanted for the entree. John requested garlic prawns thinking this was the main course. Then the waiter asked what John would like for the main course. John answered, "garlic prawns". The waiter said, "You mean—You want garlic prawns for your entree?" John answered, "Yes". The waiter said, "You want garlic prawns for your main course?" This was strange that John would be asked twice about the same thing, but he answer, "yes". The waiter then said, "OK" and off he went.

A few minutes later a relatively small plate of garlic prawns was served to John. John thought at the time this wasn't going to be much to eat for dinner.

After serving the small plate of garlic prawns, the waiter asked what John would like to drink. John answered, "I would like a bottle of beer". The waiter said, "A full bottle?" John decided on the spot that this guy was not only a bit strange but he didn't seem to understand English too well. So he answered, "Yes, a full bottle" (what else?). The waiter brought a full <u>quart</u> bottle of beer! It seems that a <u>full bottle</u> of beer in Australia is a <u>full quart</u>. The usual size bottle, as used in America, is referred to as a "stubby".

The waiter then brought the second and much larger plate of garlic prawns to John! Now it was beginning to sink into John that the real goofy one was really not the waiter. The not too understanding strange person was actually on John's side of the table.

The prawns were good, so John ate the second plate as well. The beer was a little too much, so a little of that had to be left. Garlic filled burps were the order of the day for the next two days, after that fine meal with its significant misunderstandings.

One other misconception caught John and Carol completely off guard. While walking down one of the more crowded main streets in the business district of Melbourne, people kept bumping into them. They were given dirty looks and being scowled at, and then the people would continue on their way. John and Carol were completely dumbfounded. They were really quite concerned about this and were scratching their heads trying to figure out why this was happening over and over. They finally realized they were the ones in the wrong. Unconsciously, they were walking on the <u>right</u> side of the sidewalk while everyone else was walking down the <u>left</u> side. The Australians automatically walk on the left side of the sidewalk, which is the same as they drive on the city streets. John and Carol were walking on the right side unconscious, just as they would in America. Another, "first-time-in-the-country-for-these-dumb Americans", problem was solved.

Little differences were bothersome to John and Carol at first, such as light switches. All lights are turned on by lifting up on the light switch and turned off by pushing down on the switch, right? Wrong! This is not true in Australia! The light switch is pushed down to turn the light on and up to turn it off. John and Carol were starting to realize things really were a little different here in Australia after all.

Door handles in America are located at a convenient height, so they can be easily reached. In Australia they are higher from the ground than John and Carol were used to. Australian friends later advised this is so the little kids cannot reach the doorknobs.

One difference was confounding to John and Carol for several months. They noticed something was wrong with the way the car lights shined on the road, but they couldn't determine what was wrong with them. The light appeared to be somehow different but both John and Carol were not sure why this was. After several weeks of driving, it suddenly dawned on them that driving on the left side of the road requires the dim lights to point to the left, not to the right, as they do in America. A much better feeling was had for driving in Australia after this was discovered.

Shopping was entirely different for John and Carol in Australia, particularly when they first arrived in the early 70's. During this time there were few supermarkets which were large enough to stock all of their grocery needs. Shopping meant going to several stores and they were not use to this. Fruit was bought from the fruitier, meat from the butcher, canned goods from the grocer, bread from the bakery, milk from the milk bar, and cheese and cold cuts from the delicatessen. All stores closed at noon on Saturday and there was absolutely no shopping of any kind on Saturday afternoon and all day Sunday.

Back at work one day, one of the executive managers of HDH called on the telephone and said, "John, how would you like to go to the Pitwater Wine Tasting and Food Society dinner tonight?" Boy! John thought, this really sounds like a pompous affair. John didn't know if this was going to be the sort of entertainment activity that would be interesting to him because it sounded so pompous. On the other hand, a most generous offer such as this could not be turned down. John accepted not knowing what was in store. He knew this was the politically correct thing to do, and an evening of pomposity could be suffered through if necessary, just to do the right thing. Boy, did John have the wrong slant on this whole thing!

The HDH manager picked John up at his hotel and drove him to the restaurant located many miles away in the north end of Sydney, along the ocean road. High on a hill facing the ocean sat this lovely open-air restaurant. What more could be asked than this beautiful location for a great restaurant. The bright blue of the ocean was a brilliant contrast to the white sandy beach below, and the Spanish style building superbly complemented this magnificent setting.

Greeting everyone at the front door were several men dressed in formal tuxedoes and their ladies dressed in long evening gowns. All were standing talking in small groups, while holding their white wineglasses by the base of their long stems. A sip of the wine was taken now and then, in what to John seemed to be a very pompous manner while the conversation continued a little longer. Thoughts were running ramped that this just may not be John's cup of tea.

The pompousness reflected at first impression lasted only for about 15 minutes and then everyone began to feel the effect of the white wine and all began to loosen up considerably. Soon laughter was coming from all quarters of the room.

After the round of introductions to the members and their ladies, all were led into the dining room where the seating was at a large "U" shaped table. Four types of red wine were served with dinner adding much to the four white wines served before dinner. The chef brought out the main course and paraded it around the table for everyone to see. He explained how the various dishes had been prepared, how the meat was cooked, how the gravy was made, and the like.

The wine master stood up and described what the four red wines were, how the grapes were grown this particular vintage year, and how the sun and rain had affected their growing during the season.

The cheese master stood up and told how he had visited the caves in Roquefort, France in order to select this outstanding cheese. He had been successful in talking them out of a quarter brick of real Roquefort cheese that he could take back to Australia for the Wine Tasting and Food Society. He explained how the caves were naturally at a constant temperature, which was just right for the fermenting of the cheese, and how the mold in the caves gave the Roquefort cheese its distinctive flavor, as well as its exterior color.

The Roquefort cheese was then distributed to the diners in small packages wrapped in tissue paper and tied with a ribbon. John placed one of these in his jacket pocket to be taken back to Melbourne so his wife Carol could have a taste of the real authentic Roquefort cheese. Trouble began to brew!

The coffee master stood up and talked about the coffee beans and how they were blended in order to achieve this distinctive taste.

Of course, during these talks by the various masters, everyone at the table was more than sampling the four types of red wine. As the glasses became nearly empty, other full glass magically appeared at each plate. This recharging of the wineglasses went on all through several courses of one of the most outstanding and delightful meals John had ever experienced. The room became louder and louder with laughter coming from all sides of the room.

Pretty soon the members began to stand up, one by one, and talk about how he or she liked the wine, didn't like the wine, liked the food, etc. The individual speeches became funnier and funnier as the evening wore on. By the end of the evening, John's side was aching from all the laughter. He even managed to get to his feet and make a small speech of his own telling everyone what a good time he was having with newly found friends that really knew what dinning was all about. He expressed how the food was outstanding, the coffee was great, the cheese was superb, and if the excellent wine did not stop flowing so rapidly there were going to be many people sitting around the table that may or may not make it home tonight. All in all, it turned out to be one of the best evenings John had ever experienced.

John's mind was changed forever concerning preconceived notions about pompous sounding names. After this event, it became a ritual for John to arrange his travel to Sydney on the last Thursday of each month, just to participate in these monthly dinners. Aside from learning a great deal about good food, cheese and coffee, a tremendous amount was learned about fine wines and about the people who care to drink them.

Upon arrival back in Melbourne the following day, John hung his suit coat with the cheese in the pocket in the bedroom closet. Trouble was about to begin. The excellent and authentic Roquefort cheese directly from the fermentation caves in France was completely forgotten.

Weeks went by, during which an occasion did not arise for John to wear that particular suit with the Roquefort cheese in the pocket. The weather turned hot, as January and February will do in Australia. The temperature rose to 90 and then to 100 degrees Fahrenheit and stayed there for much of this time. In the meantime, the cheese in John's jacket pocket was definitely becoming riper. Something began to smell quite badly in the bedroom!

To combat this awful smell, Carol took all of John's shoes out and sprayed them with deodorant. This didn't seem to help to get rid of the, by now, most God-awful smell coming from somewhere in the bedroom. All the clothes were emptied out of the closets and aired in the outdoors. This was no help either. The smell continued and continued, and seemed to be getting increasingly worse. About this time an occasion arose for John to wear this particular suit with the cheese still in the pocket.

Trouble did not surface while John was putting on his pants. When putting the coat on, it was a different story. The extremely bad odor suddenly became over powering. Right then and there John realized something was drastically wrong. He became aware he had forgotten the package of Roquefort cheese in his pocket. Reaching into the jacket pocket John pulled out a handful of green goo that smelled something terrible.

John immediately threw the over-fermented cheese away and washed the pocket several times with soap and water. This did little to remove the smell. Carol took the jacket to the dry cleaners. The owner of the dry cleaning plant said he had to dry-clean it twice before the smell could finally be completely removed

So much for rare cheese. Carol wasn't all that happy with the incident either, but after a while began to see the humor in it.

John returned to Sydney and the Pitwater Wine Tasting and Food Society dinners many times after that. Much was learned about some of the finer things of life. He stayed away from the cheese trays for several visits though.

During the business trips to Sydney, flight training was continued in a Piper Cherokee 180. The Australian system was just enough different from the American system for it to be necessary for John to take instruction. He enrolled in ground school also in order to become as proficient as possible with this different system. John spent many evenings at the airport after work.

FLIGHT IN THE GREAT AUSTRALIAN OUTBACK

John and Carol had a lot of time on their hands during their first Christmas period in Australia. There was little to do. They had met few Australians at this point, and of course, all the family and most of their friends were still back home in America. It looked as if the Christmas holidays were about to become the loneliest time of the year. The factories were all closing down during this period, so a bit of extra time was about to be experienced. Exploring some of the vast areas of Australia seemed to be in order to offset this lonesome period of time.

John and Carol visited the nearest travel office and handful of tour brochures were brought home. The travel agent suggested taking a bus/camping tour to the center of the continent. This was felt to be one of the more interesting and exotic travel vacations in all of Australia. A trip to the "Red Center" was eventually booked. This turned out to be a fantastic adventure.

The "Red Center" of Australia is the real Outback. Final destinations of this tour was to Ayres Rock and then on to Alice Springs. This was to be a one-way bus ride of 1600 miles, during which time they were to be served all meals on the way and would be camping out overnight in tents. 1100 miles of this was going to be on <u>unpaved dirt track.</u> They were to fly back from Alice Springs to Melbourne at the completion of the tour.

Nine days were spent traveling to Alice Springs. The tenth day was spent flying back to Melbourne. The entire trip turned out to be the most interesting and unusual tour John and Carol had ever been on.

It is curious to note that the majority of the Australians live in seven cities. Most of these are large and quite congested. Outside the cities the population is very scarce. The desert area of the Outback, seems to be way beyond the horizon and hardly even sensed by the people in the cities.

When traveling in the Outback, John and Carol became aware for the first time that there were tens of thousands of square miles of vast, empty desert making up nearly the entire interior of Australia.

The reddish colored unpaved dirt track traveled was constructed simply by a bulldozer with a large blade on it scraping across the desert to make a track. The road is generally smooth, but some areas had soft sand bogs. These had to be crossed at maximum speed to keep from becoming stuck in the soft red sand. Crossing these at a rapid clip often made the bus slide sideways which didn't do much for the comfort of the passengers. Had the bus became stuck in one of these, it would have sat there for a long time before help came along. There was virtually no other traffic to be seen in either direction for hours at a time.

Most of the area in the Outback is so remote and is such a hostile environment that there were virtually no people living in it. Only one or two cars were seen during the entire day, either coming towards the bus, or going in the same direction. Dozens of abandoned cars were seen along the track which brought home the danger of being too careless in this vast inhospitable unforgiving desert.

Crossing this vast dry desert was extremely hot inside the bus. The temperature during the day ranged between 105 and 110 degrees every day. Seldom was a cloud seen in the sky. The bus driver advised he had 20/40 air conditioning on the bus. This sounded pretty good to John and Carol until they were informed, "I will open 20 windows and try to drive as close to 40 miles per hour as possible". Unfortunately, the bus was not air-conditioned and it became swelteringly hot the majority of the time.

One of the most fascinating events along the way for John and Carol was to see the Aborigines. As the drive proceeded north further into the desert, small groups of "Abos" began to be seen. There were a number of small towns, spaced sometimes hundreds of miles apart, where they were often seen. They appeared profoundly different than any other race of people John and Carol had ever seen.

One evening, the Aborigines came near the tents that had been set up for the bus load of people to sleep in. They were selling their goods to the tourists. A number of trinkets were brought from them. All were handmade and painted with ocher. John and Carol bought a digging stick and several small hand carved figures. When they asked how much these items were, their answer was always, "two bob – two bob". The Abos didn't seem to know the real value of money. The price by them was always quoted as "two bob", no matter how valuable the item was. This meant 20 cents. "Two bob" is a hangover from the English pound sterling currency previously used in Australia.

The Aborigines could not converse in English, but they certainly knew what two bob meant. A five-dollar bill was given to them for the items John and Carol bought, expecting to get change in return. The Abo being dealt with grabbed the bill and stuck it directly in his pocket, and said, "two bob-two bob". This was such a surprise and the situation was so humorous, the Abo was allowed to keep the bill without any further fuss.

The Aborigine are primitive beings trapped in a changing civilization around them. Their children seldom wear clothes. They are semi nomadic and go "walk about" and travel several hundred miles seeking food or seeing their relatives initiated into manhood and womanhood. They speak little English, and except for a few drawings, have no written language. There are 1500 different tribes throughout the Outback. Each has their own language. They cannot talk to each other, as they do not have a common language. The tribal laws and legends are passed down to their children by word of mouth, and are often shown in their ancient drawings. Stories are told through their tribal dances.

The Aborigines play a spectacular musical instrument, called a didgeridoo. This is a primitive musical wind instrument, similar to a hollow pipe. It is played by blowing into one end, puffing out the cheeks, and continuing to play while breathing in. The cheeks press the air out at the same time a new breath is being taken. A continuous sound is made in a manner similar to that of a bagpipe. It provides an eerie, haunting tone that is never forgotten, especially when heard in the vast open spaces of the Outback.

A didgerido is made from the branch of a tree, which is quite often not straight at all, but generally has curves or may even have a severe bend in it. They are generally four to six feet in length, and have a hole cut through the center from one end to the other. How in the world is this hole ever cut down through the center of this curved tree branch?

An ingenious method of cutting the hole through the center of the didgerido has been used by the Aborigine for centuries. It is hard to imagine how a hole can be cut through the center of a curved branch, particularly without some sort of super sophisticated tool. The Abos have made this quite simple. The branch is cut from the gum tree and one end is placed in an anthill. The ants eat the inside of the branch, where the wood is the tenderest. A continuous hole through the center is created.

Beliefs by the Aborigines are profound. Included in their ceremonies for the men are ceremonial boards. These are wooden boards usually between six and eight inches wide and about four feet long, which are painted with Aboriginal designs. The women are excluded completely from the men's ceremonies and are strictly forbidden to cast their eyes on the ceremonial boards. If they do, they will die! They profoundly believe this.

Evidence of this strong belief by the women was demonstrated in Melbourne during the time John and Carol were there. Seldom was an Aborigine seen in Melbourne; however, occasionally there were a few that traveled this far south, away from their normal area of wandering.

The museum in Melbourne had a number of ceremonial boards, and perhaps without thinking or realizing their significance, these boards were put on display in one of the museum windows. Two Aborigine women walking down the street passed the windows of the museum and saw these boards. Two days later they were both found dead. Their beliefs were so strong they were said to have expired from this cause.

Seven days after the start of the tour to the Red Center, the bus carrying John and Carol and 38 other tourists, arrived at Ayers Rock. The flat vast country surrounding Ayers Rock was the typical rust-red color of the entire Red Center. The entire bus load of people walked about three miles around the base of the rock. This was only about half way around this huge rock. Several caves were explored which had Aboriginal paintings in them. These fascinating figures drawn had weathered thousands of years. Many of these paintings dated back 20,000 years! Not 2,000 years, but 20,000 years!

The next day the entire bus load of people climbed to the top of Ayers Rock. The climb was smooth and steep, particularly the first 600 vertical feet. Higher up on the rock the climb became flatter. The rock rises 1100 vertical feet from the floor of the desert and was six miles around the base. Even during the early part of the day the heat became intense. The climb was arduous enough without the added uncomfortable heat and there were many puffs and pants on the way to the top. All who began the climb from John and Carol's tour group, including several elderly people, made it to the top. All received pins when arriving on top proclaiming "I climbed Ayres Rock". Mountains could be seen 125 miles in the distance. The view was well worth the climb. The climb began at 8:00 A.M., during the cool of the morning. By 9:00 A.M., the temperature had already reached 90 degrees and was destined to go to 110F.

The climb to the top of Ayres Rock is very arduous. When John and Carol are asked if they climbed Ayres Rock they respond by saying, "Yes, twice. The first time and the last time!"

It seldom rains in this area of the Center. Some of the local communities had not seen rain for as long as ten years. When it does rain, Ayers Rock has a phenomenal amount of water running off of it. This runs down the sides in large waterfalls. Surprisingly, the rock has a number of water ponds surrounding the base that appear to be permanent. This was perhaps one of the things that attracted the Aborigine to this area. There was ample water for them to drink whereas in most parts of the Center there is not.

Drought in the area of the "Red Center" is known to be common. One of the worst in recent history occurred from 1956 to 1966. During this period of eleven years, it did not rain a single drop. Heat waves as long as 160 days were common during this drought, and the temperature was recorded as high as 113 degrees F. Nights were said to have been very cold with temperatures as low as 14 degrees F. The temperature was known to change 99 degrees within 12 hours. During this drought, most of the cattle being raised on the large "sheep stations" died.

Two seasons are known in the "Red Center", summer and winter. Summer is very hot with warm nights. Winter is also very hot with cool nights. The "wet", when it occurs, creates the monsoons between November and March. The "dry" consists of cloudless, hot days from April to October, and then it gets even hotter. One of the locals said, "When it rains here it's a mistake".

The tour continued the next morning from Ayers Rock to the Olgas. This was a distance of about 25 miles. The Olgas are a series of large rock mounds which are quite similar in color to Ayers Rock. Each is the size of a small mountain. A large number of these are in an area of about eight or ten miles in diameter. The rock formations are equally as fascinating as Ayers Rock, with the wind and water erosion creating all types of formations on the sides of the rock walls.

Both Ayers Rock and the Olgas are located in perfectly flat, desert country, without any reason for being there, except they are. There were a number of theories concerning how the Rock came to be there, but none of them seemed to be plausible to John and Carol.

John and Carol completed their tour of Ayres Rock by taking a flight in a six passenger Cessna. The front right-hand seat was available so John being a pilot managed to talk the pilot into allowing him to sit there. Discussions concerning flying began immediately and the pilot learned that John had flown a number of airplanes just like this one. There was one other couple on board the airplane.

The air tour began by a flight over Ayers Rock, then to the Olgas 25 miles away, and then on to King's Canyon which was 60 miles further north.

All were enjoying the ride over the perfectly flat desert. Naturally, John talked about some of his flying experiences. It turned out the pilot had taken instruction from the same instructor at Huxton Park near Sydney that John had and the bond was complete.

The pilot allowed John to fly the airplane for quite some time. This was a big thrill for him. A large airplane like this had not been flown for a while. The pilot pointed out a "'v'"-shaped hill in the distance and told John to head the airplane toward this. This was about the only visible landmark on the entire flat, trackless desert. Since there were no navigational aids in this area, except one short range ADF, the majority of the flying had to be done by dead reckoning.

The pilot took over as Kings Canyon was approached. Several passes were made over the interesting scenery, and then he turned the flying of the airplane back to John with these words, "Now find your way back to the airport"! Heading back over the perfectly flat terrain, after all the twisting and turning over the Canyon, with no landmarks and no navigational aids to go by, was about to be a real challenge for John.

John pointed the airplane toward the direction he thought Ayers Rock must be. John had remembered the bearing he had been flying as he was flying toward Kings Canyon. He calculated the reciprocal to this bearing and headed the airplane toward that direction, hoping the wind was not strong enough to push the airplane off course too much. There didn't seem to be too much wind, so maybe with luck this reciprocal bearing would take them back to Ayers Rock. Nothing but flat trackless desert could be seen out the front of the airplane.

15 minutes later the pilot said he was going to turn the ADF on and see how far off course John had flown the airplane. They were getting closer to Ayers Rock but it could not be seen yet. Perhaps there were landmarks there for the trained eye, but John could not pick any of these out.

The ADF needle began to swing and centered right on "0". This was a big surprise to John because this indicated the airplane was on a direct course for the airport and wasn't off one degree! This was a particularly fun and exciting experience of Outback navigation for John.

When arriving in the area of the airport, the pilot instructed John to descend to pattern altitude, fly upwind half way and cross the landing strip, lower the wheels and flaps and enter down wind for the landing. This John did. The pilot then said, "OK, you take the airplane down to the last 50 feet on final, and I will take over and make the landing." This was all a big thrill for John. A good team was at the controls of the airplane and all went well. John made a smooth and gentle approach and the pilot took over at the last moment and made a perfect whisper landing.

The bus tour continued the next day to Alice Springs. Suddenly the desert disappeared and a beautiful oasis emerged in front of the bus. The lush green city contrasted sharply with the surrounding barren desert.

The Todd River winding through the center of Alice Springs was flowing for the first time in many years. Normally it was nothing but a dry creek bed with just a few billabongs here and there. It had rained just prior to their arrival and it was actually flowing.

John and Carol learned that a "billabong" is a pool of water left over from a dried up riverbed. It can be either a pond, or a dry river that fills with water during heavy rain. In one of the Aborigine's tribal languages, "billa" means river and "bong" means dead. These billabongs vary in size from small puddles to large lakes. The name is quite often confused with the term "billy". John and Carol also learned that a billy is a bucket or can with a handle on it for making tea over an open fire. When the tea has boiled, the bucket is swung around in a circle over head to settle the grounds to the bottom.

Each New Years Day the citizens of Alice Springs turn out for their annual boat race. Of course the river had no water in it and is usually completely dry during this time of year. Holes are cut in the bottom of their boats. The participants step into these holes, hold the boat up, and each team runs like heck down the dry riverbed toward the finish line. This year the race had to be canceled because there was too much water in the riverbed.

A number of interesting places were visited in Alice Springs including Simpson's Gap, Stanley's Chasm, the Royal Flying Doctor Service, and the Alice Spring's School of the Air.

The Royal Flying Doctor Service was particularly interesting to John and Carol. It was the only medical service available to nearly the entire Outback, which consisted of hundreds of thousands of square miles. This service had been in continuous operation since 1920 and provides the only medical aid in an area two-thirds the size of the US. It now has 15 bases, twin-engine aircraft, a large staff of doctors and nurses, radio operators, pilots, and aircraft engineers. Funding is by donation and government subsidy. Patients are charged based on their ability to pay. About 40 % of the patients are Aborigines.

The Alice Spring's School of the Air was also an interesting place to visit. It provides education to children living in the Outback, who otherwise would not have schooling opportunities. Lessons are a combination of radio transmissions, correspondence courses, once per week "private" radio sessions, and at least one annual personnel visit. During the personnel visits, a light airplane or heavy vehicles would swoop in with the teachers on board. They would spend a few hours with each student and then leave to go perhaps hundreds of miles to the next student.

John and Carol and the rest of the tour reluctantly returned to Melbourne the following day, bringing their wonderful tour of the Outback to a too abrupt end. This had been the most interesting and unusual tour they would ever be on.

MELBOURNE, AUSTRALIA

SYDNEY, AUSTRALIA

AYERS ROCK FROM ABOVE

THE VERY UNUSUAL AND ENCHANTING AYERS ROCK
WE CLIMBED IT TWICE – THE FIRST TIME AND THE LAST
TIME

LOOK CLOSELY AT THE WHITE FIGURE DIRECTLY ABOVE
THE WATER

THE OLGAS

ALICE SPRINGS, NORTHERN TERRITORY

OUR BEAUTIFUL MOTEL IN ALICE SPRINGS
TWIN GHOST GUMS AND A BILLABONG NEAR ALICE
SPRINGS

CARS, TRAINS AND PLANES TO AUSTRALIA'S TOP END

During the early 1970's the three main aircraft companies in Australia, Hawker de Havilland, Commonwealth Aircraft and Government Aircraft Company and many of the smaller companies doing business with Boeing closed for a full month for the Christmas holidays every year. This provided a period of time for John and Carol to spend traveling to many different locations in this exotic land.

Areas of the Outback previously seen were very impressive so another trip to this area was planned using a different mode of transportation. The plan was to drive the car to Adelaide, place the car on the train going to Alice Springs, then rent an airplane and fly from Alice Springs to Katherine and then onward to the furthest northern city in all of Australia, Darwin. This would be a 2,300 mile trip from South Australia, thru the Australian Northern Territory to Darwin located in the extreme northern end of Australia.

400 miles were driven the first day to Adelaide, arriving just in time to load the car onto a flatbed railcar and to go aboard the train called the "Ghan".

The Ghan's personnel directed John and Carol to drive the car up a loading platform and onto the railcar. The wheels of the car were immediately tied down so the car could not move while the train was in motion. Shortly after climbing aboard the passenger train, this railcar was coupled to the passenger cars and the train pulled out of the station. One of the most fascinating adventures John and Carol had ever been on was about to begin.

The Ghan is a very impressive train. The ride is exceptionally smooth and extremely quiet. Rail construction in Australia is quite different from than in America, primarily because there are very few soft wood trees to make ties from. Australia's ties are called "sleepers" and are made from cement. The steel rails used are called ribbon rails and each is one mile in length. They are transported to the rail site being built by a special train which is one mile long. The rails are welded together which eliminates the seams. Because of the cement sleepers and the ribbon rail, the train does not sway and the train riding over them makes very little sound. There is no clickity-click sound that most other trains make. The ride is outstanding and it hardly seems the train is moving since there is no sideways movement and almost no sound.

A private compartment had been reserved which had two very comfortable swivel seats for day use, two berths which folded into the wall and a private shower and toilet facility. A dinning car is located near by which serves excellent meals. The evening meal is top notch, including a fine Australian wine and a tasty desert. All is included in the basic fare.

The trip from Adelaide to Alice Springs took from 4:00 PM the first day until 11:00 AM the next morning. After dinner the first evening the berths were unfolded and it was possible to lie down and still see out the windows. John and Carol found this all very relaxing and pleasant to rest and view the desert scenery passing by.

Several kangaroos and emus were seen along the way. This is an unusual sight since these animals are very shy, similar to the North American deer, and are seldom seen when driving in the bush..

The further north the train went the hotter the outside temperature became. Upon arrival in Alice Springs at 10:00 AM in the morning the temperature had already raised to over 100 degrees. Fortunately the humidity was very low. Further north the humidity is about to become much higher and the temperature much hotter.

Since John and Carol were going to be traveling by car over the extremely hot and dry desert, plastic gallon jugs filled with water were previously place in the trunk of the car. Many stories had been heard of people who had become stranded in the Outback and had perished from lack of water. Carrying there own water was felt to be very prudent. Five jugs were placed in the trunk of the car for safety purposes.

Shortly after arrival in Alice Springs the flatbed railcar was uncoupled from the train and moved to a ramp for offloading the cars. Once the tie downs were unhooked and the car was driven off the flatcar, John and Carol were about to explore Alice Springs, the Northern Territory's second largest city and its surrounding area.

After exploring the beautiful tropical oasis of Alice Springs and its very hot surrounding desert area for a couple of very interesting days, John and Carol drove the car to the airport and traded it in for a 180 Horsepower Piper Cherokee. This was to be used for the next leg of the trip to Darwin. The car was left in storage at the airport so it would be available for the return trip.

INTENSE DESERT CROSSINGS FOR THE UNINITIATED
ALICE SPRINGS TO KATHERINE, NORTHERN TERRITORY

The vast desert of Central Australia is considered by many to be one of the most inhospitable and unforgiving locations on earth. Being lost or stranded in the Outback can no only be traumatic, but death can result in an extremely short span of time. Water is the culprit. There isn't any! In many areas, water cannot be found in any direction for hundreds of miles.

John and Carol were about to make a flight of hundreds of miles over this vast, uninhabited, inhospitable desert. Had they realized just how hostile this vast desert region actually is, in all probability this flight would never have been taken.

Flying in the Outback is considerably different from the norm and certainly is not similar to the usual flights John and Carol were use to. Most previous flights taken in America had been completely foreign to flying over the remoteness of the Outback.   During the early 70's, when making this trip, there were few navigational aids of any kind in most of the Northern Territory of Australia. The exception was a very few ADF's (short range Automatic Direction Finders). There were only two of these in the area of this flight and they are located many miles apart. Both are located at the airports of the two cities planned to be visited

The range of the ADF's is only about 25 miles so these are to be of little value for their cross-country flight. There are no VOR's (Very High Frequency Omni Directional Range) stations and no Loran (Long Range Navigation) stations servicing the entire Outback. GPS (Global Position System), the satellite system in wide spread use today, is not even heard of until many years later.

The majority of their flying time would have to be accomplished by drawing a line on an aerial map and following its direction. Estimating and adjusting his heading for the wind and flying by dead reckoning, with only the assistance of the directional gyro compass was going to be the only method of navigation for John. There are no other navigational aids available and the flight from Alice Springs to Katherine was to be over 400 miles of nearly featureless and waterless desert.

The only major landmark capable of being seen from the air is the highway from Alice Springs to Katherine and on to Darwin. This highway was built during the Second World War by the Americans. Unfortunately, it did not parallel the straight line route from Alice Springs to Katherine. It would be a much longer flight if it was followed.

John decided to fly directly to Katherine rather than take the longer route along the highway. This was chosen even though this route over the almost featureless desert did not provide a visual reference to the direction of the flight.

This was perhaps not one of John's better decisions and it was about to create somewhat of a tense flight. The entire area, nearly all the way from Alice Springs to Darwin, is a vast, level and mostly featureless expanse of desert. The distance from Alice Springs to Darwin is 960 miles and is all untracked red sand and desert brush nearly all the way.

The first leg for John and Carol was going to be to Katherine which is 460 nautical miles from Alice Springs. There are no towns and no airports and not a single great feature to guide their direction on this leg of the flight, unless the highway is followed.

It is going to be 110 degrees along the way and if an emergency landing has to be made there would not be water anywhere on their direct route of flight. Fortunately, Carol had the sense to place two gallon jugs of water into the baggage compartment, just in case of an emergency.

This flight was going to be a real challenge and perhaps John didn't fully appreciate this in the beginning. The first leg from Alice Springs to Katherine was about to begin. John's navigational and dead reckoning abilities were about to be taxed to the utmost.

Shortly after take off from Alice Springs, the voice radio and the ADF became virtually useless. This would remain so until approaching within approximately 25 miles of Katherine.

Total distance from Alice Springs to Katherine is 460 nautical miles which would require a little over 4 hours flight. This, with a reasonable reserve of fuel, was at the high end of the capacity of the airplane John and Carol were going to fly. The reserve fuel should be adequate in the event of a strong head wind, or if the airplane is blown off course and does not track directly to Katherine. John felt the margin of safety concerning sufficient fuel with and adequate fuel reserve was within the allowable range.

During the entire first leg to Katherine, not a single crossroad, major land feature, or a single living soul would be seen. No topical features could be identified on the aerial map supplied by Flight Service. The only exception to this was the highway. This could be seen for a short period during the early part of the flight. Even then it was difficult to determine position in relation to their progress north. The highway angled to the east away from their track and after a few minutes flight could not be seen.

The outside air temperature was 105 degrees nearer the ground. Fortunately the air was very dry and even though it was extremely hot, it was not too uncomfortable at the higher elevation inside the airplane.

Climbing to 7,500 feet, the airplane reached cooler air. The temperature was still 80 degrees, but not the 105 degrees nearer the ground. This elevation of 7,500 feet was the best for flying their non-supercharged engine airplane. Above 7,500 the air would become too thin for best engine efficiency. Any higher than this, the power would diminish and cause the ground speed to decrease. This would cause the engine to burn more fuel and in an extreme case could cause the flight to be terminated short of their destination. The Outback is no place to run out of fuel!

There was little or no indication what direction the wind was blowing. It was difficult for John to determine what effect this was having on their flight. His concern was the wind may be pushing the airplane off their intended track. And it could also be holding the airplane back and increasing the rate of fuel burn.

John sensed the airplane is being pushed off to the west. He would have to do something to determine exactly what it actually was doing. John's comfort zone would have been much greater if the airplane was equipped with GPS, but unfortunately it was about 25 years too soon for this system to be developed and available.

The only real comfort was the knowledge that a turn to the east would result in an eventual crossing of the major highway going north and south. If for some reason the highway was missed, the flight could continue for hours without anything being seen until the airplane ran out of fuel. Consequences of this would be extremely severe.

There are many stories about people who have been lost in this featureless desert. Most have perished from the extreme heat and their inability to locate water. Many have become completely dehydrated, suffered heat stroke or heat exhaustion and have expired and became mummified within three or four days. This was not a very comforting thought, but it began to creep into John's consciousness as the flight continued.

The Aboriginals have learned to live with these extremely harsh conditions. They have developed the capacity to survive while traveling hundreds of miles on foot across this vast empty world of extreme heat, desert brush and sand.

An incident occurred to a group of Aboriginals as a result of being stranded while driving an old rattletrap of a car across this desert. Their car broke down. Two of them died, but the rest of the group survived by covering themselves with sand during the intense heat of the day and walking at night. They were found wandering nearly 100 miles from their car.

John and Carol had heard some of these stories prior to making this flight. The smart thing to do would have been to recognize the extreme danger being faced and not even attempt to make this trip. Ignorance normally plays a big part of foolishness, but in this case the dangers had been heard of. Were they being foolish? The consequences could be very deadly but John felt confident they could keep this flight in the safe range.

The airplane had been flown for nearly an hour with virtually nothing to point the airplane at. The directional gyro compass had to be relied on, but the heading flown would have to be adjusted for the wind. It was time for John to determine what the wind was doing to their track. A few degrees off course could result in being miles off when approaching Katherine.

John took readings several times during their flight by making a bank to the right until the airplane was flying directly north. He would fly this heading for five minutes. In all cases the wind pushed the airplane off their northerly heading by several degrees to the west. The airplane heading was then adjusted several degrees to the east to compensate for this.

John had determined the wind was coming from the north east. He turned the airplane 90 degrees to this direction and flew for 5 minutes. Keeping the nose of the airplane pointing in this direction and guiding on a small knoll, he determined the wind had blown the airplane approximately ½ mile during this time. He mentally calculated the wind velocity to be 12 miles per hour. For ease of mental calculations John assumed the wind overall had been blowing 15 miles per hour.

This meant the airplane was being held back by the head wind an equivalent of 60 miles during the 4 hours of flight. This he calculated would then require and additional half hour of flight in order to reach Katherine. John mentally estimated the total flight time required to reach Katherine considering the headwind would be 4 hours 30 minutes.

During the preplanning of the flight John had calculated the time required to reach Katherine, with no headwind, would be 4 hours. He had previously leaned the fuel flow to 75% power which would allow flight duration of 4 hours and 54 minutes. At this rate of fuel burn there would only be 14 minutes of usable fuel remaining in the tanks upon reaching Katherine. This would not be enough of a safety margin.

This was a little too close for comfort. John leaned the fuel flow even further to 65% power. This would allow the airplane to fly a total of 5 hours 15 minutes using the remaining fuel but would reduce the flying speed to 100 knots. It was going to take a little longer to get there, but the remaining fuel reserve would be greater at this power setting.

The flight continued for another 20 minutes. Still nothing was seen of the City of Katherine or the highway leading to it. Adrenaline was creating tension for John as the remaining usable fuel could become critical. Had they missed Katharine? John had done everything he knew how to do to conserve fuel and to generate the safest possible flight.

John turned the airplane straight east in hopes the highway could be found quickly before passing Katharine without seeing it.

The left tank suddenly ran dry and the engine began to sputter. John and Carol's heart began to palpitate very rapidly.

John turned on the fuel pump and the fuel line was switched to the right tank. The engine coughed twice. Then coughed once more and came back to life. This was of little consequence; however it always caused a little tension when it occurred. The real concern was that there was only one hour of fuel left in the right tank. Was this going to be enough to get them to the airport?

The flight continued for another 15 or 20 minutes on this easterly bearing and the highway was still not intercepted. The view out the front was nothing but flat desert. Were they beyond Katherine? John didn't think so, but he did not want to indicate to Carol that he was concerned.

A type of diversion was created in order to somewhat hide his concern. She was asked to keep a close eye out for the highway in order to keep her occupied.

The left tank had already run out of fuel so there was now only about 30 minutes of usable fuel remaining in the right tank. If Katherine was not found soon, they would have to make a forced landing on the highway. This was not the most desirable but it was perhaps the safest plan if they did ran out of fuel.

Carol's sharp eyes spotted something ahead. It appeared to be a group of trees perhaps 20 miles farther on. There was a straight line going to it that could possibly be the highway.

The trees ahead looked like an oasis, so a slight turn was made and the airplane was headed straight for whatever this was. Upon approaching closer, the ADF needle began to flicker and finally moved and centered on "0", indicating the airplane was directly on course for the Katherine airport. The radio also came to life with calls being made by other airplanes in the area. The trees turned out to be the City of Katherine.

A few minutes later the highway was reached and Katherine could be seen. Excess altitude was purposely maintained, just in case the engine did quit. If it did, there was a possibility of gliding far enough to reach the threshold of the runway and be able to make a safe landing. Anything was better than having to chance an emergency landing on the desert floor. John estimated there was only another 15 minutes of fuel left in the right tank.

John made an announcement over the radio to all other traffic in the area notifying them an emergency landing was about to be made of a "fuel critical airplane". Also it was indicated that a straight-in approach was being made for an immediate touch down. The airplane was pointed straight toward the threshold of the nearest runway as let down was being made in preparation for the landing. The runway was still several miles in the distance.

It seemed as if the airplane would never reach the threshold of the runway. The minutes seemed like hours. The power was cut back to idle so the engine was just barely turning over and a near gliding final descent was made toward the runway. At any moment the engine was expected to sputter and die. Fortunately it kept running until arriving over the threshold and the airplane was able to drop down onto the runway.

Wow! What a relief! They were down!

John taxied the airplane into a parking spot without further incidence. The airplane was tied down and the nearest air-conditioned motel was headed for in a taxi. The temperature had reached 110 degrees – and a very big sigh of relief was breathed. The strain of this flight was completely exhausting.

On the return trip John vowed that things would be done a little differently. The flight would be planned to fly close to the highway enough to keep it in view, even though this would increase the length of flight a little farther. Going this direction, perhaps the wind would be helping rather than hindering the progress, as had been the case on the northern flight.

Enough flying had been done for awhile. The plans were revised to take a mini vacation while remaining in Katherine for the next few days. A little time to recover from the stress of the previous day's flight was needed and this was a delightful place to do that very thing.

That evening, after a delightful and relaxing swim in the motel pool, John asked the proprietor where the best restaurant in town was located. He advised a very good Italian restaurant fairly close by the motel.

This was a very good choice and an outstanding meal was served. A ferocious rainstorm hit the city just as it was time to leave the restaurant. This kept everyone inside for a few minutes as it passed over. Lightning flashed and thunder was loud enough to almost lift everyone off their seats. Even though this was desert country, it was the "wet" season, and the rain came down harder and heavier than ever seen before. All the patrons waited in the restaurant for a few minutes until the storm passed. Several inches of water fell in just a few minutes and the walk back to the motel had to be across a number of deep puddles. It was lucky this lightning and severe rainstorm did not hit while John and Carol were in the air. Lightning is not to be trifled with in an airplane.

Before leaving on the next leg of the trip, the aerial maps were studied closely and topographical features were found that would make the rest of the trip very much easier. The route to Darwin was almost directly in line with the highway, and the distance was about half that flown from Alice Springs to Katherine.

A bit of a late start was had the following day. The takeoff time was 10:00 AM. By this time the temperature had reached 110 degrees and the humidity had increased substantially from that at Alice

Springs. The takeoff roll with full fuel and a lot of baggage was very long and the airplane didn't want to climb very fast once in the air. It took nearly 30 minutes to reach the chosen altitude of 8,500 feet. At this higher elevation the temperature cooled of a little, however it was still 80 to 90 degrees inside the airplane.

Katherine Gorge is located immediately outside the city of Katherine. The countryside had changed from the red-brown desert to a green savannah of trees with yellow sand visible between the heavy forestation. The cut of the gorge through the trees was very distinctive from the air.

The gorge is a miniature Grand Canyon with very steep red rock walls leading down to a series of lakes. John made a turn from the direct route of the flight in order to fly over the gorge. It must have been about 50 miles long as it took 20 minutes to fly from one end to the other. The view was spectacular with all the various shades of red in the rock walls, contrasting with the bright blue water in the bottom of the gorge with green gum trees on both sides. Several tour boats could be seen on the water.

Since the gorge consisted of a series of lakes with dry land in between each one, the tour boats were taking people from one end of each lake to the other and then the people would walking from one lake to the other and get into a different boat. John and Carol could see this was necessary to do in order to go thru the entire series of lakes.

Since the flight today was going to be considerably shorter and much less nerve wracking, the course was altered in order to fly over the Escarpment. These gigantic cliffs had been heard of and it was decided to see what they were all about.

They were not disappointed. The sandstone Escarpment, or cliffs, form the edge of the Arnhem Land Plateau. It is several hundred feet high and is 370 miles long. During the "wet", water cascades off the Escarpment in spectacular waterfalls. Aboriginal rock paintings have been found in rock caves along the Escarpment that have been carbon dated to have been painted more than 20,000 years ago.

They learned later that all visitors to this area were required to obtain a permit provided by the Aboriginals. Arnhem comprised the entire half of the Top End of Australia and is entirely controlled by the

Aboriginals. They apparently are very reluctant to provide permits to enter this area because of its extreme remoteness and harshness. John and Carol did not go into this area on their flight. They had flown just outside this area along its western edge. Later on in years, even flights over this area were restricted completely.

The forming of this huge rock formation called the Escarpment is not known. The favored explanation is that a massive earthquake created it. The east side of the landmass is much higher that the west side. The part John and Carol flew near is a cliff elevated into the air several hundred feet. Lush tropical vegetation surrounds the cliff on both sides and it appears as an impenetrable jungle. Waterfalls flow off the top in several places, apparently from the rainstorm the previous evening.

A forced landing in this are would be absolutely disastrous. After a few minutes John turned the airplane northwest and headed for Darwin.

Kakadu Nation Park is located 75 miles southeast of Darwin and was flown over. The airplane had to be raised higher than 2,000 feet above the ground because the National Park is a game preserve. What appeared to be several hundred thousand large birds could be seen everywhere, but mostly on the ground. This was so impressive from the air that John and Carol planned to rent a car the next day and drive back to this fantastic Park.

While traveling toward Darwin, but still in the Park area, John and Carol could see hundreds of large mounds on the ground, spaced very close together. They were termite mounds. There were literally thousands of them. It was later learned the mounds quite often reach a height of 50 feet and are as big around as 20 feet in diameter. There had to be millions and millions of termites in each mounds. It was a very impressive sight. Obviously, there are many times more termites in the area than there are people in all of Australia. There could even be more termites here than there are people in the world.

Traveling at Christmas time in the Northern Territory of Australia is perhaps not the wisest thing to do. The temperature is always the hottest of the year and Darwin was experiencing an exceptionally hot and humid heat wave. Even the local people were complaining.

Upon arriving at the airport, the temperature as 112 degrees and the humidity was absolutely over powering.

THE TOP END – DARWIN AND KAKADU PARK

Upon arrival in Darwin a taxi was taken to the apartment previously reserved. The flight from Katherine, with the few side sightseeing trips, had taken most of the day. On the way in their taxi, a shopping center had been spotted located about three blocks from their apartment. Something for dinner was needed so a walk to the shopping center was in order.

Walking out the door of the apartment into the high heat and humidity was like someone had thrown a bucket of hot water on them. After walking just one block, it was doubtful John and Carol could make it the rest of the way to the shopping center. This was a real surprise. The heat and especially the high humidity is extremely oppressive and it became necessary to stop and rest every so many feet. Several attempts were made before the remainder of the short walk could be completed.

A few groceries were bought and carried back to the apartment. The return trip was no different. This was a great struggle causing a number of short walks to be made along the way.

It was decided that a bus would be taken into town and an air-conditioned car would be rented. It was going to be nearly impossible to be outside in this extreme heat and exceptionally high humidity. Things got better after this, but it was still necessary to spend most of the time inside the car, with very quick and very short sojourns outside.

John and Carol explored the city of Darwin for a few days and took in all of the attractions. One of them was exceptionally interesting. It was a visit to the crocodile farm. It was very exciting to learn more about these strange, ancient creatures. The area of the farm was fenced off in a manner that permitted people to be on one side and the crocs to be on the other. Several different water areas were on display. Some of these had hundreds of small crocs in them. Others housed groups of very large ones.

The gamekeeper fed the crocs while standing inside the enclosures. When a croc became a little too friendly and started toward him, he very hurriedly threw another chicken toward it. The crocs fought over these, ripped them into pieces, snapped up a piece and swallowed it whole. This was not a good place to be standing and it made them realize just how dangerous they were.

The grand daddy of all crocs was housed in a very large pool by itself. This particular crock was 22 feet long and weighed more than two ton.

The gamekeeper fed this very large croc by holding a chicken over his head. The gamekeeper was about six feet tall and his arm placed the chicken at least 8 feet above the water surface. Nothing could be seen of the crock below the water until he suddenly jumped out of the water toward the chicken. That 4,000 pound croc jumped out of the water and took the chicken right out of the gamekeeper's hand. Had he not dropped it about 4 inches as the croc snapped it up he just might have been minus a few fingers or even half an arm.

The next day John and Carol jumped in the rental car and drove to Kakadu National Park. On the way the mounds seen from the air were stopped at. Most of the mounds were about 20 feet tall and perhaps 30 to 40 feet in circumference. Millions of termites lived in each one.

The termites are very clever little insects. Somehow they are able to orient their mounds in such a way they become air-conditioned internally. The sun hits one surface and creates a wind draft through the mound. This starts at the bottom and continues up through the mound to exit out the top. The temperature inside the mound is kept considerably below the air temperature outside.

Much of the Kakadu Park is covered with water, either in billabongs or in swampy fields. Most of the swampy fields are completely covered with magpie geese. The geese are smaller than the North American Canadian Honker. They are about the size of a large chicken. They are colored black and white and resemble a large magpie. It is astonishing to see the huge number of them in a field.

John and Carol made an estimate of their numbers by counting a small segment and then multiplying their count by the entire size of the field. Their estimate totaled well over 200,000 geese in just one field. There were many, many more fields with just as many geese in them.

Several large rock outcroppings along the side of the main road were highlighted by signs indicating each was an ancient Aboriginal living site. John and Carol left their car and walked about a quarter of a mile on a path through thick brush to get to each of these. They were very interesting to see, but the short walk in the oppressive heat and very high humidity made returning to the air-conditioned car as quickly as possible almost a must.

Aboriginal paintings are located on the walls and in the shallow caves of each rock outcropping. The paintings are still very vivid even though they had been painted between 5,000 and 20,000 years ago. Most are of animals. Emus and kangaroos can be recognized. Some are more map like, seemingly telling stories of the routes to take to the next watering hole, etc. They are all very fascinating and each one is a little different from the other.

There are very few hotels or other developments in or near this unspoiled vast Park. John and Carol did find one that had rental cars. At the advice of one of the Park Rangers, they were able to trade in their rental car for a four-wheeled drive jeep. A side trip into the Outback country to a place called Jim Jim Falls was planned and the road and trail in was described to be too rough to drive their original car into. The Ranger was not wrong as they later found out.

The Four Seasons Kakadu Hotel, where John and Carol traded their vehicles is very unique. It had been built in the shape of a crocodile. It is a very expensive first class hotel. The locals indicate,

"You enter through the mouth, you eat in the stomach, and you pay thru the nose".

Jim Jim Falls is a very beautiful waterfall, which drops several hundred feet off the top of the Escarpment into a small lake. The falls are surrounded by very thick, lush tropical vegetation.

The way to the falls is the roughest trail John and Carol had ever driven over. It was rough going even for a four wheel drive vehicle. The first 10 miles is a very, very rough road. A sign indicated the next six miles is classified as impassable for vehicles of any kind.

The sign was not completely ignored; however they felt by driving very slowly the trail could be negotiated. Very large rocks located at several places on the rough trail were gone over at a slower than walking speed. A four wheel drive vehicle is the only type of vehicle that could possibly make it, and it was doubtful even this could make it back. One area had a very large rock that had to be driven over the top of and straight down the other side about three feet into a mud hole. It was doubtful this could be negotiated on the way back because it was going to be necessary to drive straight up this rock. There was no other way around it.

Very little time was spent at the falls. The air was stifling from the heat and very heavy humidity. There were signs all along the way saying not to swim or get too near the water because crocodiles live in this area. It was not necessary to be warned twice. A hurried picture was taken out the window of the jeep and a turnaround was made to head back almost immediately. It was a bit of a struggle, but after three tries, the face of that large rock was negotiated without high centering. Wow!

Only one other couple was seen on the entire trip to the falls. They were hiking! This would not have even been considered in this crocodile infested land and in this heavy, heavy humidity.

The next day a boat trip was taken on a very large billabong. This in America would be called a lake it was so large. Here it is known as the Yellow Water Billabong.

The guide pointed out several crocodiles along the way. All that could be seen above the surface of the water, if they could even spot them, was their two eyes and their two nostrils. The boat was able to get within five or six feet of one. It wasn't even visible until it jumped out of the way and swished it powerful tail at them. It had to have been at least 16 feet long as it was as long as the boat John and Carol were riding in.

John and Carol returned to Darwin the next day and traveled around in order to learn something of the history of the city.

They learned that Darwin was nearly annihilated during the Second World War. The Japanese bombed it in 64 different air strikes.

After several enjoyable days in Darwin, the airplane was flown back to Katherine and then to Alice Springs. This time the highway was followed all the way and it wasn't nearly so nerve wracking.

Arriving at Alice Springs, the car was taken out of storage at the airport and the very long drive back to Melbourne was begun.

When traveling this route previously the road from Alice Springs to Melbourne was a dirt track. Fortunately, a modern paved highway had replaced this in the interim.

Much later and after John and Carol had visited the city, on Christmas Eve 1974, Cyclone Tracy nearly annihilated the entire city a second time.

A cyclone in the Southern Hemisphere is the same thing as a tornado in the Northern Hemisphere, except it blows in the opposite direction. Sustaining winds during the cyclone of 1974 reached 180 miles per hour, and lasted for 5 ½ hours.

From the newsreels seen at the time almost every house was blown right down to its foundation. It looked as if an atomic bomb had flattened the entire city. There wasn't a building left standing for many, many blocks.

The chief acceptance pilot for Qantas Airlines, who had become a business acquaintance of John's, had flown a 747 into Darwin the day after the storm and brought out load after load of people. He flew them to Townsville, on the east coast of Northern Queensland. These flights currently hold the record for loading more people on them than any other flight in history.

The armrests on the seats of the airplane were raised and seven people were loaded into a four-seat assembly. All were strapped in. No baggage was allowed on board. All these people were forced to leave with only the clothes they had on their backs.

The airplane was lightly loaded with fuel as the flight was a short one for a 747. Even with more than twice the normal load of passengers, the airplane was significantly under its maximum gross weight limit. The entire city of approximately 80,000 people was evacuated in this manner.

Reconstruction began right away. No one was allowed to go back into Darwin until the city was rebuilt. Several ships were moved into the harbor and anchored. These were used as hotels for the workers rebuilding the city. The large generators on board the ships were used to generate electricity and supply the reconstruction effort.

FLIGHTSEEING MOUNT COOK, NEW ZEALAND

In Australia and New Zealand the winter seasons are quite short. There was little opportunity for John and Carol to go skiing, which had been one of their principal athletic endeavors in the past. The season begins in July and ends in August.

During the first winter in Australia, John and Carol decided to fly to New Zealand for a ski vacation. They scheduled a week of skiing at Cornet Peak near Queenstown, and then a second week of touring by bus around the South Island. This ended at the world famous Hermitage Resort Hotel on the side of Mount Cook. The trip culminated with a flight in a small plane around and over Mount Cook which is the highest mountain peak in the southern hemisphere.

Their trip originated in Melbourne with a flight to Sydney on Qantas Airlines. Then a local airline was taken to Christchurch. From there another flight was made on a commuter airline to Queenstown. Their skiing accommodations for the first week were in a nice 300-room motel on the edge of Queenstown.

The city of Queenstown nestled into a valley surrounded by mountains on one side and a large lake on the other. A shuttle bus provided transportation to and from the ski area and was a spectacular ride as it serpentines around the side of the mountain. Many sheep could be seen on the valley floor hundreds of feet below and on the sides of the gentile mountains. They appeared like hundreds of grains of white rice on a green carpet.

This was the first skiing John and Carol had done this season. It was also the first skiing they had ever done during the month of July. The end of the second day found them ready for a break. The next day became a day of rest and shopping in Queenstown.

The city of Queenstown is located in a picturesque setting on the edge of Lake Wakatipu. On the opposite side of the city from the lake and within walking distance of the downtown area is a shear mountain cliff rising 500 feet nearly straight up. A gondola lift located at the base of the cliff takes people to the mountain lookout restaurant located on the edge of this shear cliff.

The gondola is quite unique. It split into two halves for loading and unloading. The ride to the top presents an ever increasing spectacular view. From the precipices of the restaurant's large picture windows, the view of the city far below, with the lake and mountains in the background, is spectacular nearly beyond description.

John and Carol's next adventure was a boat tour to a sheep station on the opposite end of the lake from Queenstown. While loading on the boat, two young men were also seen going aboard. John and Carol couldn't help noticing them because of their extremely scruffy appearance. They had several days' growth of beard, matted hair that appeared not to have been washed for several weeks and old ragged clothes that had long since seen a washing machine. Their appearance was so bad everyone turned away from them. Upon arrival at the sheep station, it was discovered these two young men were the entertainment! They were the sheep shearers. Their appearance was certainly in character and they really put on a good show.

An interesting demonstration of the sheep dogs was also provided. The dogs were phenomenal. The handlers turned the dogs loose and sent them about a quarter of a mile away. They were so far away they could hardly be seen as they ran. The dogs were never spoken to. Hand signals alone were used to indicate which way they were to go to find the sheep. Once they found the sheep and were herding them back toward the handlers, the dogs were not directed at all. They automatically brought the sheep straight back to the handlers. The sheep were then herded by the dogs into a small pen.

A handler indicated to one dogs that he was to go from one side of the pen to the other. Instead of running around the sheep to get to the other side, the dog jumped on the sheep's backs and ran across by jumping from one to the other. John and Carol were absolutely amazed and really impressed with the entire presentation.

The chief handler explained the dogs were never played with. A particular handler would train and handle each dog. No one else was allowed to handle or work them. They are considered working investments and not pets. Their cost is extremely expensive and range in the thousands of dollars for each dog.

After skiing for a week and sightseeing in the Queenstown area for a few days, a small commuter airline was taken to the Mount Cook area located on the northern part of the South Island. The airliner landed at the base of the mountain and the passengers were driven by van to the Hermitage Lodge.

John and Carol received their first glimpse of Mount Cook as the commuter airplane arrived. It was most impressive with few lower mountains around it and no higher mountains obstructing the view. This mountain pretty much stands out by itself and reaches from the peak directly down several kilometers to the ocean.

The first sight of the lodge is as spectacular as the first view of the mountain. Located a few miles up a valley, it virtually sits on the edge of a glacier. All the advertisements say this is "the Lodge with the Million Dollar View", and it surely did have that! The view from the lodge front windows was of Mount Cook with its rugged cliffs, peaks, glaciers, and snowfields and is just about as spectacular as it possibly can be.

Mount Cook is located 15 miles from the Tasmin Sea and the base is only 1,000 feet above sea level. There are no high mountains close to Mount Cook, so the view is unbroken virtually from sea level to more than 12,000 feet at its summit. More of this mountain can be seen at one glance than most other major peaks in the world because of this factor.

There are many hiking trails spiking out in all directions from the center of the Lodge. Many lead into the surrounding mountain valleys and continue up the mountain side.

John and Carol took several short day hikes along one of the smaller glaciers close to the Lodge. The view was spectacular but the hikes were not as adventuresome as they might have been. Notices along the way indicated the trails went through the valleys and eventually became "climbs not for the novice, and were not to be attempted unless properly equipped, trained, and were escorted by licensed guides."

This was brought home to them by the icefalls right beside them. The ice came crashing down making a loud rumbling noise heard for miles around. The falling ice creates small avalanches on the glacier which would be most dangerous if caught below them. The walking trail took them along side the glacier on a safe shelf above the level of the ice.

Near the end of their stay a flight around Mount Cook in a Cessna 206 was scheduled. John and Carol were picked up by the same van that had brought them to the lodge and taken to the airport at the base of Mount Cook.

They joined a small group of people waiting for the ride in the airplane. John talked to the pilot in an attempt to capture the right hand front seat again, but to no avail. The pilot had already promised this to someone else.

Shortly after takeoff one of the two major glaciers on the mountain could be seen in its entirety. The stark white of the ice and snow contrasted sharply with the exposed rock of the craggy cliffs and the bright blue sky. It was fortunate the weather was so nice. There wasn't a cloud in the sky and they were in for a most interesting and spectacular flight.

The pilot announced the glacier being flown over is the Fox Glacier. It is 13 kilometers (8 miles) long. He also told them it is 900 feet deep and the vertical fall, the altitude change from top of the glacier to the bottom, is nearly 8,000 feet.

The airplane flew up the glacier and over a ridge into the next valley. There is another glacier flowing down the opposite side. It is even longer than the first one. It is called the Fronze Joseph Glacier. The face of this begins 1,000 feet above the Tasmin Sea and extends up the mountain nearly 12 miles.

Flying around the mountain peaks was exciting to John and Carol, particularly when they were about to fly over a mountain ridge and down the other side. Not only was the view tremendous, but it appeared as if the airplane was too low to go over the ridge. It was startling for them to be flying straight toward a saddle on a ridge thinking the airplane is not going to make it over, and then to be flown right over it without any problem. This had a tendency to get their attention real quick.

As the flight continued small groups of 6 or 8 people were beginning to be seen down below on the glacier. Some of them were skiing; however, two larger groups were along side an airplane that had landed on the glacier. Its tracks could be seen in the shallow snow on top of the ice. The people had stacked their skis in one area and appeared to be getting ready for lunch. The temperature was warm enough to have their jackets off and they were standing around sunning themselves.

Our pilot told us the skiing could be quite good during certain days. Often times when the sun comes out, as it was this day, it would warm up to around 70 degrees on the glacier.

The pilots had to pick their days for taking people skiing and landing on the glacier. The amount of snowfall is monitored closely for two chief reasons. The snow cannot be too deep for the airplanes to land on the glacier, and it can not be so deep that it covers up the crevasses. The guides must be able to see the crevasses in order to lead the skiers away from them as they are skiing down. The pilot advised there is one area on the glacier that can be skied down continuously for 18 kilometers.

The airplane began to gain altitude at this point and went over the top, right next to the peak of the mountain. The summit of the mountain is 12,349 feet, so this placed the airplane 12,000 feet high. We could only stay at this altitude for a few minutes without oxygen, so once viewing the highest point of the mountain, the pilot immediately started to descend.

The airplane was so high it took nearly half an hour to descend to the airport. During the descent, the pilot flew past one of the hiking huts built on top of a cliff. The airplane was so close it seemed as if the hut could be touched by reaching out the window. The hut was perched on the top of an extremely steep ridge. The trail leading to it is so steep a mountain goat would have to hold on with all four feet.

This hut is one of several built on the mountain. The one flown past is at the 8,000-foot level and the route to it is so severe, the material to build it must have been hoisted there by helicopter. It would have been all but impossible to carry heavy material up those steep cliffs to reach this height without some sort of sophisticated equipment.

The hut is many trail miles from the bottom of the mountain. With the distance involved and the elevation from the Lodge, plus the steep terrain, John estimated it would take all day just to hike one direction to the hut. There is no level ground at the top, except where the hut is located.

It was exciting to see the hut from this vantage point inside the airplane. John and Carol both doubted it would ever be seen in any other way. The steepness of the trail is way out of most people's capabilities.

The pilot made a whisper landing on a grass meadow several miles from the airport. He landed going up a gentle hill and the airplane came to a stop without having to put the brakes on. Even though the landing area is not paved, a very smooth landing was made on the grass. Pilots who fly these airplanes really seem to know what they are doing. The magical van was there waiting to take us back to the Lodge.

This beautiful country with its outstanding mountainous terrain is magical. The next day had to be another return to reality. John and Carol jumped onto another commuter airplane to Christchurch where they met the direct flight to Melbourne, Australia.

After the flight John passed along his experiences with mountain flying to Carol. He pointed out there is a phenomenon that occurs while flying in mountains, particularly with people who have not had much experience flying in this environment. In John's early days of mountain flying, the valleys appeared smaller to him than they actually were. To make a turn around appeared to be nearly impossible. Actually there is generally more than adequate room; however, the perception tends to be off until a pilot has acquired a significant amount of mountain-flying experience. He told Carol it has taken time to become accustomed to this perception. There is always somewhat of an uncomfortable feeling associated with turning around in a valley until this perception is learned.

John pointed out another phenomenon which also occurs until becoming more proficient. Keeping the nose of the airplane level with the horizon will keep the airplane flying level. When flying directly toward a mountain, the level position of the airplane appears to be the visible horizon on top of the mountain. It is not. The level position is actually below this point. Many times it has been noticed that while flying higher than the elevation of a ridge, the airplane appears not to be high enough to make it over the top. As the airplane comes closer to the ridge, this impression disappears and it becomes obvious the airplane is actually higher than the mountain. This perspective must also be learned through experience.

This knowledge doesn't seem to make it any easier when someone else is flying, particularly when it doesn't appear the airplane will make it over the next mountain.

COMPLEX CLASS FLYING— MIDDLETOWN, OHIO

After completing his first assignment in Australia John moved on to the next assignment at the Aeronca Company in Middletown, Ohio. This assignment was particularly interesting to John since this factory manufactured the first airplane he had taken instruction in and had flown his first solo in more than 30 years previously. The airplane manufactured by them was the 65 horsepower, two place Aeronca Champion.

The Director of Manufacturing for Aeronca still had a copy of the actual drawing used to make the original Champion model. The entire drawing is contained on one page. Included is the engine, as well as the entire airplane structure. This is certainly different from the thousands of pages of drawings used to manufacture a Boeing airplane.

John's flying career had advanced as a result of flying the hundreds of hours he now had in all sorts of light aircraft. He was now flying more complex aircraft than the light Cessnas and Pipers. He was able to join the Aeronca Flying Club which owned and operated two airplanes, a Piper Cherokee 180 and a Piper Cherokee Arrow 200.

Flying the Arrow was appealing to John as it was much more advanced and had retractable landing gear, a constant speed prop, a fuel-injected 200 horse-power engine and the capability of flying very high over the top of most weather.

The club insisted that a pilot have 200 hours of logged time with 10 hours of instruction in the Arrow, before being allowed to fly this aircraft solo. It was a bit more sophisticated than the usual single engine aircraft. Since this airplane is a high performance single or complex class airplane, it makes a great deal of sense to have these restrictions in order to insure the pilot is adequately proficient. This class of airplanes requires experience and knowledge of its more complicated systems to be able to fly it properly and safely. It just might ruin a pilot's day to forget to put the landing gear down before making a landing, for example.

Flying this particular airplane was a big thrill for John. Numerous cross-country trips to interesting places were taken during his two year stay in Ohio. Quite often John and Carol would get up early in the morning and take a ride in the Cherokee Arrow before going to work.

The Aeronca factory is located on the airport where the two Club aircraft are hangered. This was convenient for John and Carol's early morning jaunts. The sunrise rides were often taken to distant airports where breakfast was being served. It was possible to make the return trips in time to go to work without ever skipping a beat.

Muncie, Indiana was the favorite destination. From Middletown, Ohio, this is a distance of 112 nautical miles. There is an excellent restaurant on the field at Muncie. It is possible to fly there, land and taxi directly to an aircraft parking spot right in front of the restaurant.

Breakfast at this restaurant became a twice-weekly ritual. Flying over, having breakfast, and flying back required about two hours. The waitresses became so used to seeing this airplane come in at the same time each morning that the orders for breakfast were placed before the airplane came to a stop. Coffee was poured and ready at John and Carol's favorite table as they came in the door.

One early morning flight resulted in a strange and different flight experience. John listened to the ATIS as Muncie was being approached. He then reported to the control tower, "Muncie Tower, Cherokee 8413 Charlie, 10 miles South, inbound for zero two zero. I have Brovo."

Use of the phonetic alphabet to title each tape transmission allowed the controller to immediately know if the pilot of the approaching aircraft has the latest up-to-date information. In this case the controller had titled the transmission "Bravo". If the pilot's transmission indicates he has the old information, the controller will give him the current data.

Muncie tower answered the call with, "13 Charlie, report five mile down wind. We are experiencing heavy traffic."

John: "13 Charlie". This indicates the tower transmission had been received and understood.

John: "13 Charlie is five miles on down wind for zero two zero"

Tower: "13 Charlie, Proceed"

Tower: "13 Charlie, what is your position?"

John: "13 Charlie. 4.2 miles DME (this indicates John was 4.2 miles from the airport as measured by the Distance Measuring Equipment).

Tower: "96 Delta, what is your position?" (The tower was calling a different airplane.)

Pilot of 96 Delta: "96 Delta 4.2 miles DME"

Boy, John thought that airplane is right where his airplane is. John said to Carol, "I don't see him. Do you suppose he is under or over the airplane, out of our line of sight?"

Tower: "13 Charlie, do you have the traffic?"

John: "Negative, 13 Charlie."

Tower: "96 Delta. What is your position?"

Pilot of 96 Delta: "3.8 miles DME, 96 Delta."

Tower: "13 Charlie. What is your position?"

John: "3.8 miles DME, 13 Charlie."

That aircraft was still right in the same location John's airplane is, but for some reason John couldn't see it. This was beginning to be nerve wracking since the other airplane had reported twice in the exact same area as his airplane. Scanning the ski in all directions, John could not see another airplane anywhere.

Tower: "13 Charlie, maintain two five zero zero"

This instructed John to remain at 2,500 feet which is 500 feet above the traffic pattern. This would hopefully separate this airplane from the other one by approximately 500 feet. This is not much distance between the two airplanes, and if one has a different altimeter setting, the two airplanes could be right on top of each other. Both aircraft had to be traveling in excess of 110 miles per hour. At this speed things could happen fast if something should go wrong. This thought did not help John's nerves. Where is that other airplane?

Tower: "13 Charlie, what is your position? Do you have the traffic?"

John: "13 Charlie. 3.2 miles DME at two five zero zero. Negative on the traffic."

Tower: "96 Delta. What is your position? Do you have the traffic?"

Pilot 96 Delta: "96 Delta. 3.2 miles DME at pattern altitude. Negative on the traffic."

Listen to that! That other airplane is right on top of them! Scans were made again in all directions, under the airplane, over the airplane and on both sides. Still no other airplane could be seen. John pulled the throttle back and the airplane slowed to just above the stall speed.

Tower: "13 Charlie. What is your position? Do you have the traffic?"

John: "13 Charlie. 2.6 miles DME at two five zero zero. Negative on the traffic."

Tower: "96 Delta. What is your position? Do you have the traffic? Are you two traveling together?"

Pilot of 96 Delta: "96 Delta 2.6 miles DME at pattern altitude. Negative on the traffic. Negative, I am flying alone."

Where the heck is that other airplane? Nothing could be seen anywhere.

Tower: "13 Charlie. Position and traffic". The controller's voice seemed to rise in volume and was almost an octave higher than normal.

John: "13 Charlie. 1.4 miles DME at two five zero zero. Negative on the traffic."

Tower "96 Delta. Position and traffic"

Pilot of 96 Delta: "96 Delta. 1.4 miles DME at pattern altitude. Negative on the traffic."

This was getting to be intense! Every time a position was reported to the tower, that other airplane reported exactly the same position. That airplane had to be above, below, or in back of this airplane but seemed to be nowhere. Changing airspeed more than what had already been changed could possibly cause the two aircraft to collide in mid air. It was apparent John's airplane could not be seen by the other pilot either. Both aircraft must be traveling at the same speed in order to be at the same location over and over!

Tower: "13 Charlie. Descend to pattern altitude and proceed. OK to land. The traffic is approaching from the opposite end of the runway."

What a relief! It was impossible to determine where that other airplane was in relation to John's. His location was reported exactly where John's airplane was every time. This was disconcerting since it appeared the other airplane had to be out of his vision, perhaps directly under John's airplane. Scans were made in all directions and the other aircraft just could not be located. The tower controller must have been a little confused as well. He apparently couldn't see him either, as the other airplane reported the identical distance from the airport as that of John's each time. His aircraft had to be traveling the same speed, but was actually approaching the airport from the opposite direction. In actual fact, he was miles away and was not a threat. Another whisper landing was made and a pleasant breakfast was had before returning to go to work.

A few days later a vacation was scheduled and John and Carol flew the Arrow to Nashville, Tennessee, to see the Grand Ole Opry. This is a distance of 250 nautical miles and requires a flight of about two hours each way.

The Grand Ole Opry had little appeal to John and Carol before making this trip. They had watched it a number of times on television, but it seemed of little interest. The flight provided a reasonably long cross-country trip which offered something to do different than the usual short flights that were being made around the Ohio area.

The plan was to fly to Cornelia Fort Airpark, which is a non-controlled airport in Nashville. It is located fairly close to the Grand Ole Opry grounds and a taxi could easily be taken from the airport.

Cornelia Fort was named after a lady who was one of the outstanding pilots in the WASPs (Women's Army Service Pilot) during World War II. She had flown and ferried warbird aircraft from the factory they were built at to their Air Corps destinations. She had flown nearly every type of fighter and bomber to air fields throughout the US, Alaska, Canada, Mexico, and South America. Unfortunately, she was killed in a freak accident. Her contribution to the war effort was such that her hometown named the airport after her.

John and carol located a motel near the Grand Ole Opry grounds. A shuttle bus ride was available from the front door to the main entrance of the grounds each morning.

The first morning, just as they where getting off the bus and walking toward the entrance to the Opry grounds, John received a tap on his shoulder. The man doing the tapping asked if John would like some tickets to the Grand Ole Opry for that evening. John thought, "What kind of a come on is this?" The man said, "These are free. I have had two extra tickets for tonight's show for several months. My friends couldn't make it, so if you would like them, you can have them". Because they were quite expensive tickets, John asked what he wanted for them. He said, "Oh no, I don't want anything for them. You can have them for nothing." Two tickets were handed over and he said, "I'll meet you at the show" and then walked away.

John figured this just had to be some kind of a scam. He suspected the man would demand money for them later, since the tickets appeared to be for the more expensive seats. The man did say he was going to meet them at the show. Maybe he would put the bite on them then.

John bought entrance tickets to the Opry grounds and they entered the main gate. The grounds are an amusement park with rides and amusements. There are small theaters located here and there. Each theater has a fifteen or twenty-minute shows every hour throughout the day. Little thought was given to the "free" Grand Ole Opry tickets for that evening's main performance.

In addition to the small theater entertainment, groups of musicians were playing on several street corners in the park. They played for a few minutes and then moved to a different corner and another group would take over their spot.

After a few minutes of this, the visit was really beginning to be enjoyed. The musical groups were made up of big name musicians that were actual members of the Grand Ole Opry. The sidewalk and small theater entertainment continued all throughout the day. John and Carol had both lunch and dinner on the Opry grounds. The evenings Grand Ole Opry main show was about to began at 8:00 PM.

John and Carol entered the theater, showed the tickets to one of the hostesses and were escorted to their seats. The tickets were for seats in the very front row of the theater. This couldn't have been a better location since the theater held 6,000 people. It looked to John like this venture was going to end up costing a bundle!

The man who had passed the tickets along to John and Carol arrived a few minutes later and sat down next to them. He introduced himself as a man from Kentucky. He lived just across the river from Cincinnati, which was fairly close to where John and Carol were living in Middletown, Ohio.

John could see that the tickets were quite expensive, so he offered the man the price marked on the tickets. He would not accept the money and would not consider a smaller amount either. In fact, he would not take money for the tickets at all. This was a complete surprise to John since he had expected the worst.

The evening show of the Opry was nearly three hours long, and was one of the best-organized shows John and Carol had ever seen. The numerous entertainment acts moved one right after the other with no hesitation during nearly all of the three hours.

The show was being televised continuously. During the commercial breaks, the commercials could be heard, but the activity on the stage was halted. The MC remained on the stage and a number of front row people, such as John and Carol, jumped up to talk to him during the breaks. Porter Wagnor was the MC for this show. Several people ran up and shook his hand while pictures were being taken. This was exciting too, as all of the MC's were well known personalities who were on television for the Opry.

John and Carol had planned a late dinner after the show. John invited their benefactor for the tickets to come along. He felt this was the least they could do for such a generous act.

At the late dinner, John tried one more time to pay something for the tickets. The man absolutely refused to take anything at all.

The entire Grand Ole Opry activity was enjoyed much more than John and Carol had anticipated and it would be re-visited any time, should the opportunity present itself.

Outside the main gate of the Opry grounds is the Opryland Hotel. This is a superior five star hotel. It has nearly 3,000 rooms, three swimming pools, 30 specialty shops and an 18-hole golf course. This is by far the most magnificent hotel John and Carol had ever seen anywhere they had traveled.

The hotel was constructed into several wings. The interior of each wing is an open courtyard. The balconies to all the rooms face inward, overlooking beautiful gardens with walkways meandering through lush shrubbery, flowers, trees, over bridges and across running streams. Each court is different and each one is magnificent.

There are 8 ½ acres of courtyards inside the hotel. Each wing has a different theme. One is oriental with Japanese pagodas, walkways and trees. Another is tropical with palm trees, hibiscus flowers and volcanic rock.

Each wing has 10 floors of rooms on each side. The open courtyard is actually covered with a transparent roof. This lets in the natural light and makes it appear as if the courtyard is open to the outside.

A buffet breakfast was served each morning in one of the courtyards. The view from the breakfast table is over a beautiful garden. The wrought iron room balconies overlooking the courtyard provide the appearance of the French Quarter in New Orleans.

The hotel was a very pleasant place to have breakfast, and then stroll through the various courtyards, gourmet and high fashion shops. John and Carol had a delightful morning wandering around this wonderful hotel.

The short holiday ended all too soon. In the early morning, John and Carol found themselves in a taxi heading for the airport.

After preflighting the airplane and proceeding through the checklist, "clear the prop" was sounded and the engine was started with the usual bang of thunder at the first turn over. Takeoff into the light breeze took John and Carol over the grounds of the Grand Ole

Opry and directly over the Opyland Hotel. It was surprising to see just how big the hotel really was.

Shortly into the flight back to Middletown, John ran into a rainsquall. The visibility was greatly restricted by huge raindrops hitting the windshield. A 90-degree turn was made and the flight was diverted around the rainsquall. That was about the only excitement on the entire return trip. The airplane wasn't really being diverted back to Nashville as was suspected by Carol the copilot. The rain was just an isolated shower, and the remainder of the way home remained clear.

SPECTACULAR HELICOPTER RIDE— HAWAIIAN STYLE

The most unusual and spectacular helicopter flight experienced by John and Carol took place in Hawaii, on the island of Kauai. This particular island is quite small but outstandingly beautiful with its profusion of flowers. There are so many flowers along side the main roads it is difficult to take a meaningful picture.

John made a return trip from Australia to Seattle at least twice a year for business purposes. On one of these turn around trips from America back to Australia, John and Carol took a short vacation. Since Hawaii is a normal stop on the way, it was a shame not to take advantage of a few days in this tropical paradise.

Upon arriving in Kalaheo, the largest city on the island of Kauai late one evening, John and Carol discovered there bags had gone to Maui. Fortunately, the airline returned them to Kauai early the next morning. They were delivered to the door of the motel in time to make themselves presentable for breakfast.

After a delightful early morning swim in the ocean, John rented a car and they began to tour the island's north side. They drove along the coast as far as they could go. The road ended at the steep cliffs along the western end of the island where they were not able to go any further. The countryside along the way is tropical with palm, banana, mango and other tropical fruit trees, as well as pineapple, and sugar cane fields. A profusion of flowers is everywhere, making it a most delightful and relaxing drive along the ocean.

A lovely ocean lagoon was driven by which had an extremely dark shade of blue water. Elvis Presley filmed the movie, "Hawaii Blue Lagoon" at this location.

John and Carol spent all day driving down to the western end and back on this beautiful north side of the island.

Arising early the next morning, they had a swim in the ocean again and then had breakfast of tropical fruit, while sitting in the open air restaurant, overlooking the lovely palm tree studded beach and brilliant blue ocean. Work was a million miles away.

The next day's excursion found the ocean highway along the southern part of the island was even more spectacular than the northern route. The first exhibit was a blowhole cut by the water in a rugged part of the ocean shoreline. When the large breakers hit the blowhole, the water spouted like a geyser, sending water and foam 50 to 60 feet into the air.

The "Grand Canyon of Hawaii" is located near the western end of the south side of the island. This is much deeper and more colorful than expected and is carved right out of the mountainside. Several waterfalls could be seen in the distance up through the canyon while driving on the highway.

While stopping for lunch, some local people provided directions to a magnificent local beach. This is completely isolated from the surrounding countryside. A rough road is the only way in, and the beauty of the pure white sand offset the palm trees making this a pleasant tropical setting. Not a single person was on this lovely isolated beach. John and Carol had the entire beach to themselves for the entire afternoon.

Next day, since the only two major roads on the island had already been explored, something different was chosen for diversity. A helicopter tour of the island was scheduled for early morning. This was considered to be quite expensive so John and Carol had second thoughts about going, but having little else to do decided to go anyway.

John had previously been given a description of a helicopter by a friend who was a staunch fixed wing pilot, "A helicopter is a collection of rotating parts going round and round, and reciprocating parts going up and down, all of them trying to become random in motion. Helicopters can't really fly – they're just so ugly the earth repels them".

The helicopter flown that day was a Bell Ranger, which carries four passengers and the pilot. Each of their party had an outside seat, which was perfect for both sightseeing and taking pictures. As the helicopter climbed away from the airport, the beauty of the bright blue ocean contrasted vividly against the multi-colors of the flowers and palm trees. What a striking sight at low altitude this was as they were taking off.

The flight along the southern coast was glorious and was awe-inspiring as the "Grand Canyon" of Hawaii was approached. When they reached this area, the pilot flew the helicopter deep into the crags of the gorge and up face to face with a huge waterfall. He hovered so close to the waterfall the water could almost be touched had they put a hand out the window. The spray could actually be felt coming into the cabin of the helicopter through the air conditioning system. He then zoomed the helicopter over a ridge and down the other side into a deep canyon, up to the top of the mountain, and down the other side into another canyon. The ride was spectacular, and cameras were clicking rapidly as several rolls of film were used in record time.

When they left the area of the "Grand Canyon" the pilot dropped the helicopter down to the surface of the ocean. He cruised so low to the water it appeared John and Carol's feet were about to get wet.

At the extreme western end of the island, the flight continued quite low, near the surface of the ocean, until they came to the steep cliffs. The helicopter was faced directly toward the cliffs and was raised slowly to take full advantage of the spectacular view. Once over the top of the cliffs, the mountainous area came into view. There is a large volcano located there which dominates the entire landscape.

The pilot of the helicopter was competent and skillful. He climbed the helicopter over the rim and then gently began to lower the big airship into the center of the volcano. It had been raining earlier in the day and water was running from the top, down the steep sidewalls inside the volcano, making seven waterfalls. He gently lowered the helicopter down into the volcano to about 700 feet from the top rim. The sight was unearthly with the waterfalls cascading down the shear inside sidewalls of the volcano from the top. The pilot held the helicopter at this elevation and slowly made two complete revolutions while hovering in mid air. The view was absolutely breathtaking! What a thrilling experience this was for John and Carol to look straight up the steep canyon-like walls and see daylight at the top, and realize the helicopter was indeed in the very bowels of a volcano. Slowly and deliberately the pilot raised the helicopter straight up. From this position in the center of the volcano, they gradually climbed to a position above the rim. From there they could see straight down into the area they had just left. The pilot told them they had climbed more than 1,000 feet to exit the volcano. They were indeed down inside a volcano a very, very long way.

After the flight was over, both John and Carol commented that it had been such a spectacular flight they would have gladly paid twice the going price for this tremendous experience.

MORE TRAVELS IN AUSTRALIA

When John's assignment completed in Ohio, a second assignment to Melbourne, Australia was accepted for a second tour of four years. He and Carol rented a beautiful home in Middle Brighton, which is a suburb of southern Melbourne.

The assignment was somewhat the same as that taken 15 years previously. Seven different companies were now doing business with Boeing in Australia so the job was even more extensive than before.

A considerable amount of travel was associated with this assignment. The traveling provided John and Carol the opportunity to see a great deal of Australia and to do a little flying along the way.

One of the longer airplane trips John and Carol made while in Australia was to northern Queensland. This was the state comprising the northeastern third of Australia. Most was tropical and the weather was at times hot and humid.

The flight was up the east coast of Australia to Brisbane and then farther north along the Great Barrier Reef. John rented a six-place, straight-tailed Beechcraft Bonanza and the expenses were split with another Australian couple who joined them. Their small son came along so there were five people in the airplane.

Departure was scheduled for early Saturday morning. The plan was to take two full weeks vacation in order to see as much of the Great Barrier Reef as possible. This was not nearly enough time to see it all, even by traveling in a small airplane, but time off from work was limited.

The original route was to have been up the coast to Brisbane, Rock Hampton and then farther north to Prosserpine, which is near Townsville, Queensland. This is a total distance of 1800 miles each way.

The Great Barrier Reef begins at Rock Hampton and extends north for more than 2000 miles. In the southern most area, it is only a few miles off shore. Farther north the Reef becomes farther and farther off the coast.

John and Carol's friend called the Australian Flight Service Station to get the latest weather report and to file a flight plan just prior to leaving. Flight Service recommended not going at this time as there was severe weather along the coast to the north.

This came as a real blow to everyone. The bags had all been packed and ready to go. John and Carol had made a stopover at their friend's house for the previous evening in order to be ready to go to the airport in the early morning. If they were to go at this time, an alternate route would have to be found.

Aircraft charts were spread out all over the front room floor. A lot of data was pored over and an alternate route was selected that was inland a couple hundred miles. This wouldn't be quite as scenic a trip as the coastal route, but perhaps the bad weather could be skirted around by going this way. Perhaps the return trip could be made down the coast.

Flight Service was contacted once more to review the weather over this new route. Much to their great excitement, Flight Service advised the route of flight should be clear all the way. Excitement reigned supreme and all were instantly ready to jump into the airplane and be gone.

A short drive was made to the Bankstown Airport. The airplane was loaded, fueled, and preflighted in record time. All climbed into the airplane and the trip was on!

Their friends' small boy sat in a car seat strapped to the rear seat. The two wives occupied the middle seats and John and his friend sat in the front as pilot in command and copilot respectively.

John would never forget the call sigh of this airplane. It was PWT (Popa Whisky Tango). The airplane had tremendous performance. With its 300 horsepower engine, it cruised at 180 knots or 207 miles per hour. A lot of ground can be covered in short order and the airplane is a dream to fly.

First stop was Brisbane. From Bankstown near Sydney the flight took four hours. All were glad to get out of the airplane and stretch their legs, as well as to keep from stretching the bladders any further.

A landing was made at Archer Field and all stayed that evening with John's friend's relatives. The next morning, after a sumptuous breakfast, all piled into the relatives car and were driven a short distance to the Gold Coast.

This area is similar to California's Marineland, except it is much larger. It has two entertainment areas which have pens built in the water of the ocean. These contain the porpoise and sea lions used for the entertainment. A water skiing exhibition was the main attraction, along with the trained porpoise, sea lions, and seals.

The water skiing exhibition was outstanding. Two skiers were towed from one boat at the same time on two different towlines. The boat driver made a sharp turn maneuver and each skier skied entirely around the boat. Both were skiing in opposite directions. This was almost unbelievable. John and Carol had to see it a second time to realize they had actually both gone around in opposite directions.

The Gold Coast is a beautiful area with magnificent white sandy beaches. A profusion of condos is just off the beach. One of Queensland's first casinos is located in the center of this small community.

The Gold Coast is the last of the commercialized areas of the Great Barrier Reef. From this point north, it has been left pretty much in its natural state. This is one of the real attractions of the Reef. Magnificent resorts are on some of the islands, but for the most part the surrounding areas around the resorts have been left completely undeveloped.

The next leg of the flight was to Rockhampton. This city is located just inside the tropics, immediately north of the Tropic of Capricorn. The weather is beautiful most of the year, with hardly a cloud in the ski, but warm. The temperature rose that day to 90 degrees F. and the moderate humidity made it quite balmy.

A motel was located for the evening that had a beautiful swimming pool with lush tropical vegetation surrounding it. A delightful evening was spent relaxing in the nice warm water in this lovely tropical place. Dinner and a couple of large tropical drinks on the balcony of the restaurant overlooking the ocean made for a very pleasant evening.

Motels in Australia are a little different from those in America. There are virtually no restaurants in Australia serving breakfast. The large hotels and the motels are the only places serving this particular meal.

Breakfast orders are placed on a multiple-choice card the night before. This is hung on the doorknob outside the door to the room. Late in the evening, the operator of the hotel or motel picks up the cards and prepares breakfast as ordered for service the following morning. This is served in the room at the time specified on the card.

A trap door is generally located directly over a small table in each room. The door has an external lock, which is opened by the motel operator when breakfast is about to be served. The breakfast tray is slammed into the room and the door is slammed shut, all in a matter of a split second. This experience is mindful of a convict receiving his meal in prison, but perhaps a little more pleasant.

Breakfast is usually cold cereal, toast, marmalade and tea or coffee, unless a larger hot breakfast of eggs, bacon or ham, toast marmalade and tea or coffee is ordered. The toast is always served unbuttered and wrapped in a serviette. The toast generally doesn't seem to have ever been near a heat source. The orange marmalade is quite good, once becoming used to it. The tea is always excellent.

Pancakes are never served for breakfast. The Australians cannot understand how we Americans can eat all of that sweat gooey stuff in the morning. Pancakes, if ever eaten, are eaten as a dessert after the evening meal.

For some unknown reason there is always one thing found on the menu that does not make sense. That is "spaghetti on toast". No one John and Carol knew or ever met seemed to think they would like this or order it. It doesn't seem to sound very good to most Australians either.

After a hearty breakfast of cold hard eggs, cold toast and delicious hot tea, a return trip was made to the airport and a short flight of thirty miles was made to Great Kepple Island. This has a lovely horseshoe shaped beach with gentle surf breaking onto it. The airport is located in the center of the island and it is just a short walk to the resort hotel and beach area.

The resort is magnificent with two large swimming pools located just a few feet from the beach. The water temperature in the ocean is nearly the same as the air temperature, which is near 90 degrees almost all the time. Strolling on the beach with a quick run and jump into the ocean gentle surf and then a quick exit out of the water into the intense tropical sun was very pleasant. The dip into the ocean, even though the water was quite warm, was very refreshing.

The tropical island with all of its brightly colored flowers, palm trees and lush vegetation is outstandingly beautiful and the resort quite grand. Being in the tropics, the 90 degree weather couldn't have been more pleasant.

The first glimpse of the Great Barrier Reef came as John and Carol and their friends were tourists in a glass bottomed boat. The ocean bottom scenery was extremely colorful. Tropical fish of all sizes and shapes were everywhere. A sea snake came to the surface for air and then darted back down into the deeper water. The sea snake is said to be one of the most deadly snakes in the world. Fortunately for man, they are docile and seldom attack humans.

Many of the beaches along the Great Barrier Reef are closed to swimming. Most beaches are posted with signs warning not to go in swimming because of the Portuguese man-of-war jellyfish. They have long tentacles often reaching 20 feet in length or even longer. A human is poisoned every place the tentacle touch his skin. Many people have died as a result of an encounter with this insidious jellyfish. Fortunately there are no Portuguese man-of-war jellyfish on or near this tropical island.

Sitting around the swimming pool in their swimming suits, sipping tall cool tropical drinks, made for a most delightful day.

When the sun became too hot, a dip in the pool or in the ocean cooled things off nicely. The rest of the world didn't even exist!

One of the locals pointed out a particular bird in a tree. He said, "Now watch this". He whistled a small tune. The bird duplicated his few notes exactly. Then he made a strange noise like the voice of Donald Duck. The bird made the same sound. Several other sounds were made and the bird immediately followed with the same identical sound. The name of the bird was told to John and Carol, but this has long since been forgotten. During all of the eight years spent in Australia, never again did John and Carol come across this bird. You don't suppose it was a hoax, do you?

The resort has several small travel trailers located a couple hundred yards down a jungle-like trail. These are rented to casual visitors. In Australia they are called caravans. One was rented and several days were spent on this magnificent island.

After swimming, snorkeling, sun bathing and just plain relaxing around the pool for a number of days, it was difficult to return to reality and fly onward to other great adventures.

After several days stay on this lovely island a flight was made to the small town of Prosserpine. There was little here except the airport and a small group of empty buildings. A car rental was located at the airport so a "sort of" car was rented. An open-air car called a Mini-Moke was the only vehicle available. This monstrosity was similar to a jeep with a canvas top and no sides. It may have been strange looking but riding around in it was pleasantly cool in the tropical heat, and it served its purpose well.

The Mini-Moke was driven to another small community located on the ocean. From there a ferry was taken to Daydream Island. This island is off the shore about 30 miles and is located directly on the Great Barrier Reef.

During the journey to the island, the crew of the ferry put a large rope net out, which was attached to a beam sticking out from the side of the ship. The lower end of the net floated on the surface of the water. John and Carol changed into their bathing suits and joined the fun by climbing down the net and holding on for dear life while being dragged over the water. The net had to be held onto with all their strength as it was being dragged through the water at about 30 miles per hour. The dragging on the rope net was exciting and the warm water was refreshing. Even though the water was quite warm, the moving air was quite cool when getting out.

Although it didn't happen to our party, the crew advised they sometimes dropped someone off and had to go back and pick them up.

During the 1½ hour trip over to the island the ferry crew held a door prize drawing. John and Carol's group won the two bottles of champagne. Since it was Christmas Eve, a supply of paper cups was found and champagne was provided to everyone. John and Carol ran around the crowd on board with the bottle in hand and passed out small drinks until the champagne ran out. Everyone was provided a small toast to the holiday. John and Carol even entered the wheelhouse and a small drink with a toast to the holiday was presented to the captain.

For this effort, the captain put his captain's hat on the ladies and had them steer the ferry for a minute or two. All were having so much fun that on the way back, somehow their group managed to win the bottles of champagne again. A bit of collusion was suspected but it provided for a good time for everyone. Since it was now New Years Eve, a repeat was made of the process of passing around small toasts to the New Year.

The beauty of Daydream Island is absolutely staggering. It is just what the advertisements all suggest. The island is small, just large enough for the resort, with a lavish tropical garden surrounding it all.

The wharf, built from the island to the navigable water, is quite long. The Reef is just under the surface of the water. The coral bottom can be seen while walking from the ferry to the beach along the wharf. Huge turtles weighing perhaps 50 to 100 pounds were swimming in the water. Many were seen while walking on the long wharf from the ferry to the island.

The Daydream Resort has a salt-water swimming pool, which is advertised to be the largest in the world. It has large rock heads, similar to those found on Easter Island, surrounding the outside of the very large swimming pool. A cocktail bar is on an island in the middle of the pool. It has a bridge extending from the side of the pool over to the miniature island. The island can either be walked to or swam to. Barstools located just under the surface of the water are available to sit on. Sitting in the water, sipping a tropical drink at the bar, surrounded by this lovely resort—it just doesn't seem to get any better than this!

This almost unbelievable, make-believe setting was difficult to leave. Returning to reality seemed out of place as they drove to the airport for the flight back to Sydney the following morning. Since the weather had improved and there was not a cloud in the ski, the route of flight was along the coast. The coast line consisted of miles and miles of white sandy beaches, seemingly going on forever. Few people were seen on them for hundreds of miles.

A number of shipwrecks were passed as the flight proceeded south toward Sydney. Most of the shipwrecks were iron ships, but occasionally a wooden hulled sailing vessel could be seen rotting away in the shallow water. These had all been wrecked and marooned as a result of striking the coral just below the surface of the shallow water.

The water in the Barrier Reef area is known to be extremely treacherous. In the early days, there were few, if any, navigation charts and those that were available were inaccurate. The viscous tides, and the even more viscous coral reefs, trapped many of the ancient mariners. Few survived a shipwreck to tell about it since civilization in those days was a long way away.

Upon arriving near Sydney, a complete circle was made around the city. This city of over four million people is very large in area and it takes more than an hour to fly around it at more than 200 miles per hour.

When arriving at the bay in front of the Opera House, Traffic Control instructed John to circle and hold until a 747 landed at Mascot International Airport. This wasn't objectionable, as a fantastic view of the down town business district of Sydney was visible, as were the waterways leading inland from the ocean.

The Opera House appeared like a large sailboat's sail as they flew over it while in the holding pattern. John held the aircraft at 500 feet above the water as directed by Flight Control. This is an unusually low altitude for an aircraft over a city, but Flight Control allowed this as most of the flight was over the water of the bay. The 747 could be seen in the distance as it passed by and went in for a landing at Mascot Airport.

Circling in this manner made the Sydney harbor seem quite small, but in fact it is quite large. Crossing it on a ferry takes well over an hour.

The flight back to the home airport at Bankstown took another 15 minutes. The flight to and from the Great Barrier Reef area had taken a total of 18 flight hours and some of the most unique and outstandingly beautiful country in the world had been seen. It had been one of the most enjoyable and most memorable trips of a lifetime

FIRST AIRPLANE PURCHASE

Some unknown wise man once said, "The two happiest days in a man's life are the first day he buys a boat and the first day he sells it." This seems to be a truism concerning airplanes as well, although the selling part can be a little emotional.

Owning an airplane has been a life long goal of John's and a much hoped for desire. The time for retirement is rapidly approaching and something is going to have to be done to create an interest in order to keep active after retirement. Operating and maintaining an airplane seems to be just the right thing to fill this need.

Many years have been spent flying someone else's airplanes. The urge to own one for himself gradually gained momentum with the passing years and money put aside to do so was about to burn a hole in his pocket.

Too many of John's friends and business associates had completed their working life with little to do in retirement. John felt he owed it to himself to create an activity in order to keep well occupied and not fall into the trap of being inactive, as so many of his friends had. It was becoming obvious that people who did not have a lot of activity after retirement tended to quickly lose their health. John is determined not to let this happen to him. Besides this is a strong argument he can use to convince his wife that buying an airplane is really the right thing to do.

During the last several years of John's working life with the Boeing Company he has been on assignment to Australia. Prior to returning home to America he had garnered enough arguments to convince his wife they should go forward with the airplane purchase. He has worked 35 years for the Company and is anxious to find out what it would be like to maintain and operate an airplane of his own. Now is the exciting time to do the one thing he has always dreamed of and that is to buy and fly his own airplane!

During the long stay in Australia general aviation activity had been followed diligently by reading the "Flyer", the biweekly newspaper published in the Western United States. The "Airplanes for Sale" section was pored over from month to month. One day an advertisement popped out at John that just could not be ignored. He just knew the airplane being advertised was going to be that special one for him.

The owner of the airplane is located in Bend, Oregon. John gave him a quick phone call. When the owner came on the line John told him he was calling from Melbourne and was quite interested in his airplane. He said, "Oh, Melbourne, Florida?" John said, "No, Melbourne, Australia." There was a long pause on the other end of the line. Then he said, "You must be kidding!"

The conversation went on for a few more minutes until he was finally convinced John truly was calling from Australia and that John truly was interested in buying his airplane.

Negotiations were begun immediately over the phone. This took a number of phone calls from six thousand miles away during the next few weeks. Finally a selling price was agreed upon. A substantial amount of money was sent to the owner for the down payment to indicate John's good intentions and to secure the sale.

For John, this is one of the most exciting things he had ever done. John now owns an airplane. Perhaps he was a little too excited because all this was done without ever seeing the actual airplane! How smart can that be? The airplane could very easily turn out to be a real dud.

John's second thoughts after completing the purchase seemed to indicate that perhaps a foolish act had just been committed. "My God, what have I done? This airplane has been bought without ever laying eyes on it. It would serve me right if it turned out to be a real dog." Somehow though it was felt this was just the right thing to do and this would turn out to be just the right airplane for him. This was strongly hoped for in the back of John's mind!

A business trip was made to Seattle a month or so after John's telephone negotiations were completed. A few extra days' vacation was taken and a drive was made to Bend, Oregon to determine how foolish John's actions had actually been. With every mile driven toward Bend, John became more nervous just thinking about how senseless this whole affair really must be. This could well prove to be the most stupid and certainly the most costly venture he had ever undertaken.

After looking at the airplane and reading the associated aircraft records closely, it was a great relief and a pleasant surprise to realize the airplane was in better condition and had more in it than there was any reason to expect.

By now, excitement was running high. After reviewing every detail about the airplane during the short time he had available, John concluded he had actually made an outstanding bargain. He had to agree though, this had to be the stupidest way of going about the smartest thing he had ever done.

The airplane was a 1976 Piper Cherokee Arrow with a 200 horsepower fuel injected engine, a constant speed propeller, and retractable landing gear. It was fully instrumented for IFR (Instrument Flight Rules). It even had an automatic pilot, a Loran navigation system and a four-place intercom. The interior and exterior were in reasonably good condition, and the color was white with red and black trim. It had a distinctive red tail.

John's emotions were like a kid on Christmas Eve anticipating the presents to be opened the next morning. Unfortunately a return trip to Australia had to be made and the airplane had to be left where it was for the next few months.

The previous owner flew the airplane to Harvey Field in Snohomish, Washington, near Seattle, shortly after John's permanent return to America. This airport would become home base for John's new airplane.

Purposefully, the airplane had been bought knowing it had a high time engine and this would have to be replaced or remanufactured soon. Shortly after having the airplane flown to home base, John made a decision to have the engine remanufactured right away.

Remanufacturing an airplane engine is an interesting process. This is accomplished utilizing original manufacturing tolerances. In most cases, nearly all the moving parts are replaced with new parts. The pistons, the rings, the cylinders, the heads, the valves, all are removed and replaced. In John's case the original crank was found to be well within the new part tolerance so this remained in the engine. The engine case was sent out for magnaflux inspection for cracks. Any found were repaired by being welded.

At one time during the overhaul, new parts were on their way from California, Oregon, Texas, Pennsylvania, Connecticut and Washington.

The propeller was removed and taken to a prop repair facility. "The prop is a very important part of the airplane. It serves as a big fan in front of the airplane to keep the pilot cool. If you don't believe this, just have it stop and then you can watch the pilot sweat."

The prop was overhauled and all new seals were installed. The engine was now "0 timed", as was the constant speed prop. Next a panel mounted GPS (Global Positioning System) was installed. The Loran system in the airplane didn't work well in the mountains, so this was upgraded to the newly developed GPS technology.

An Arnav Star 5000 GPS and a coupler that would connect the autopilot to the GPS were placed on order. After installation, the autopilot could fly the airplane and be guided by the GPS, without having the pilot touch the controls, except to hold altitude. Now all that had to be done was to learn how to use all this new equipment.

The number one principal of owning an airplane was quickly learned. "It's easy to make a small fortune in aviation. You start with a very large one." John also soon learned that, "If God meant man to fly, He would have given him more money". Aside from all that, the airplane was becoming a delight to fly and to maintain.

Since it was now several months since John had flown a complex class airplane, a few hours training from a qualified instructor seemed to be in order. Sliding down the runway on the belly of the airplane after forgetting to put the wheels down, or something equally as embarrassing, would not be in John's best interest.

After an hour or two in the air with an instructor the airplane became more comfortable to fly. Solo cross country flights were begun and the real learning began in order to use all of the new equipment in the airplane, particularly the new GPS navigation system.

Now you know the story behind one of the dumbest moves that turned out to be one of the smartest and most enjoyable things John had ever done.

THEY JUST SEEM TO FLY BETTER WITH WHEELS UNDER THEM

John and Carol began to explore the many interesting areas of the Pacific Northwest shortly after buying his new Piper Cherokee Arrow. Local trips were made in the new airplane to such places as the San Juan Islands and to other interesting places in and around the Seattle area. Flying to Friday Harbor on San Juan Island or to East Sound on Orcas Island were perhaps the two most favored. Both locations were pleasant to fly to and ideal for a most enjoyable day trip over the waters of Puget Sound. There was one particular trip that didn't turn out quite so well.

This particular trip became intense and nearly ill fated. John and Carol will remember this flight for a very long time. It would seem that a malfunction of the equipment in the airplane would not allow the retractable landing gear to go down and it was going to be necessary to land wheels up. This was something nearly all pilots think about but fortunately few of them ever have to experience.

The San Juan chain is made up of a large number of islands. Some are large and have airports on them, while others are relatively small. Navigating through them can be a little tricky if unfamiliar with the area. Having good navigation equipment, like the GPS John had installed, made this easy and pleasurable.

John was excited about using all of the electronic equipment in the airplane. The newly installed panel mounted GPS (Global

Positioning System) was a fantastic improvement over the older systems of navigation. This system was new to general aviation and nearly everyone was beginning to rave about it. Use of it made it extremely easy to navigate directly to any one of the many islands in the San Juan's. After using this new equipment for a short period, John learned that it would be difficult to be without it.

The only access to the San Juan Islands is by boat or by airplane. The people on the small communities on these islands are laid back and pleasant to visitors. The larger communities such as Friday Harbor and East Sound have top quality restaurants within walking distance from their airports. Excellent seafood is their specialty and is a good substitute for the "$100 hamburger".

The Seattle area had a lot of rain this particular early spring season and flying conditions were not the best for a number of weeks.

John was eager to fly the new airplane and to explore out of the way areas, particularly around the San Juan Islands using the newly installed equipment.

One Saturday morning the weather changed and became beautiful. The sun came out and the temperature warmed to 70 degrees. There wasn't a cloud in the sky and not a breath of air was stirring. Flight Service indicated a high-pressure area was aloft with a 5 to 10 MPH breeze blowing from the south and no rain was predicted for the immediate future. It could not have been more ideal for flying.

John and Carol fueled the airplane and quickly took to the sky, heading for Friday Harbor located on the island of San Juan. This is the largest island in the San Juan group of islands. The flight was going to be a distance of 75 miles and it would take half an hour to get there.

The clear blue cloudless sky was pleasant to fly in through the islands. Another whisper landing was anticipated with a short walk from the apron parking area to the small, tourist attraction business district of Friday Harbor.

John and Carol's favorite restaurant is situated on a hill directly above the ferry dock overlooking Friday Harbor Bay. The view from the tables located by the large picture windows is beautiful and the activity in the harbor is always interesting to watch. There is always several sailboats and powerboats coming and going, and occasionally a seaplane can be seen landing and taxiing to the wharf.

Their favorite lunch at this restaurant is pan-fried oysters. These are perhaps not everyone's favorite; however, the oysters served here are small, delicate, and are prepared in a delicious batter. The flavor is excellent and they did not have a strong, over powering oyster taste.

The restaurant is located about a mile from the airport. The walk is generally pleasant with a number of interesting shops to window shop in along the way. The distance from the airport is just enough to get a little exercise and work up a good appetite, without becoming too strenuous during the return walk back to the airport with a full stomach. Just such a pleasant couple of hours were anticipated, but this time it was not to be.

A few days prior to this flight John had been working on the airplane's interior electrical system. The overhead light fixture was removed and replaced. A switch on the dashboard controlled the interior lights. This has a rheostat that brightens and dims all the inside lights. It is used to dim the lights for night flying in order to keep from destroying the pilot's night vision. This feature was to play an important role in John and Carol's next adventure which turned unusually intense.

Flying along the shore of Puget Sound, just off the Washington mainland, was most enjoyable. The clear sky meant visibility was unlimited and a large number of islands in the San Juan chain could be seen all the way.

Summer homes dotted the shoreline of many islands. Most are quite elaborate and have private docks extending into the water. Numerous sailboats and powerboats are anchored along side several of the docks. Some homes even had seaplanes anchored nearby.

The flight had been relaxing and enjoyable up to the point of making the approach to Friday Harbor Airport. The GPS had done its job and had directed their flight straight toward the airport on San Juan Island.

Since they were flying quite low to the ground, John's let down was only about 2,000 feet and this didn't take much time. The descent to 1,000 feet above the water was made, which was pattern altitude for landing at Friday Harbor.

John began going through the landing checklist just prior to entering the traffic pattern. The manifold pressure was reduced to 21 inches. The prop was cut back to 2100 RPM, and the airspeed began to drop. Fuel was switched from the left tank to the right in order to land using the fullest tank. The electric fuel pump was turned on and the fuel mixture was pushed forward to the full on position. The prop control was advanced to full fine and the airplane was nearly ready for landing

Next to be done was to ensure the airspeed had dropped to below 150 MPH and to lower the landing gear. The airspeed was now down to 145 MPH, so John moved the landing gear lever from the gear up position to the gear down position.

Some airplanes make enough noise when the landing gear is being lowered to enable the pilot to hear it move. It was not possible to hear the gear move in John's airplane, so the lights on the dashboard had to be relied upon to indicate what the gear was actually doing. A yellow light illuminated when the gear was in transit up or down. In addition there are three green lights, one for each wheel, which illuminate to indicate when the wheels are down and locked into place.

As John moved the gear lever to the down position, the "in transit" light should have lit. It didn't come on! Now that was unusual! Then the three green lights, which would indicate the gear was down and locked, also did not come on! What in the world? Didn't the gear come down?

John raised the gear handle. The in-transit light didn't come on again, as it should have as the gear was being raised. John lowered and raised the gear handle again. Still the in-transit light and the three green lights didn't come on. John had no way of telling if the landing gear had moved down and was locked into its proper landing position or whether it had moved at all.

The gear handle was raised again and then an attempt was made to lower the gear with the emergency landing gear lowering system. John activated this by moving a lever located between the two front seats to the gear down position. The landing gear <u>seemed</u> to cycle, but the indicator lights still did not come on.

This was beginning to be a little more than just worrisome to John! Suddenly John's and Carol's interest in the anticipated lunch disappeared.

John raised the gear handle once more and applied full power to the engine and flew the airplane out of the traffic pattern. The thought of the landing gear possibly not coming down had become a major concern!

John climbed the airplane to 3,500 feet and cut the throttle back in order to lower the airspeed to below 150 MPH. He then lowered the flaps. The landing gear system was cycled again and again. The indicator lights did not come on! This was becoming more than a little concerning. John knew this could become a real incident and could even become dangerous. Without knowing if the landing gear was down and locked, a wheel's up landing might have to be made!

What would he have to do if the gear could not be lowered and locked? Would it be better to land on grass than it would be to land on a hard surface runway and grind the bottom of the airplane off! Where was a grass runway? These thoughts were going through John's head. He made a major decision to head for Harvey Field 50 miles away which, in addition to the paved runway, did have a grass runway. If he was going to have to make a wheel up landing, it would be best to do it on grass rather than on a paved runway.

John cycled and recycled the gear while traveling to Harvey Airport. The system continued to react in the same manner. Neither the in-transit indicator light nor the gear down and locked indicator lights would come on. There were no new results. The emergency landing gear system was also tried several times. Still the indicator lights would not come on. The situation was becoming more and more intense and the sweat was beginning to pop out all over John's forehead. Carol was becoming a bit concerned as well.

Visions of the prop curling on impact with the ground and dollar signs flowing out the bottom of the airplane could almost be seen if a belly landing had to be made. A prop strike on such a landing could ruin the engine and this would cost big bucks, to say nothing of the danger that would exist to the occupants.

Real fear was beginning to taker hold of both John and Carol. Should an emergency be declared at this time? This didn't seem to be the proper thing to do since the condition of the wheels was really still unknown. It was possible the wheels were actually down but the indicator lights just didn't come on. What good would it do to declare an emergency at this stage? John decided to hold off on making this decision for now.

Dick, the owner/manger of Harvey Field was called on the radio. He had become a good friend and had a great deal of knowledge of John's airplane and the way the various systems functioned.

The Intercom radio on the field answered John's call. A female voice advised Dick was at his house which was located on the field close by. He would be called on the phone and alerted to the problem.

Slow circles around the airport were flown for a few minutes and the gear was cycled several times, still to no avail. Oh how John would hate to have his nice new airplane all bent up landing without wheels.

Their safety began to be of major concern if John had to make a landing with the wheels up. John began to prepare for such an emergency. He began to go through all the alternatives and to decide what could be done to protect them as much as possible from a dangerous landing.

Carol was instructed to climb into the aft cabin area and to strap herself into the right hand rear seat. Then she was told to take one of the seat cushions stored back there and put it up in front of her. That seemed to be the best that could be done to prepare her for a sudden hard stop, if this should occur.

John began to review all the things that would have to be done if a wheels up landing was going to have to be made. The entry door would have to be popped open just before touchdown. This would allow getting out of the airplane in case the landing buckled the body enough to jam the door. A touch down going as slow as possible would have to be made. Cutting the engine just before landing and turning off the fuel and electrical supply was also planned just prior to touch down. What more could be done in order to protect themselves? All these things were running through John's mind just as Dick called on the radio.

Dick asked John to describe the problem, which he did. He said, "Dick, I don't know if the wheels are coming down or not. The lights on the dash board are not coming on. Dick said, "Let's just calm down a little and think about this. You have plenty of time and lots of fuel. We can all use this time to find the problem and fix it before trying to make a landing." His words were very soothing and everything he said made a lot of sense. John hadn't noticed before how badly his hands were shaking.

Dick said to recycle all the circuit breakers. These were all pulled out and pushed in one at a time. The gear handle was lowered again and the gear was cycled. The indicator lights did not came on.

Dick said he would go outside with a hand held radio and watch John's gear go down as he made a low pass over the airport.

The airplane was circled and a long and slow approach was made to the field. The airspeed was reduced to as low as John felt could safely fly down the runway and still be able to rise up at the other end. The airspeed would still have to be above 90 MPH which would mean going over the airport faster than John would have liked to. If the airspeed was any slower than this, it would be tempting fate. There were trees and power lines at the opposite end of the runway that would have to be raised over the top of.

The flaps were lowered all the way and the landing gear lowering handle was placed in the down position. The airplane was lowered to about 30 feet above the ground. A long low and slow pass was made directly over the runway. Dick was standing on the ramp and reported the wheels were down but he couldn't see if they were locked or not.

This presented a real dilemma and was a dangerous position to be in. If the wheels were down but not locked, the landing impact would cause them to fold. This would cause even greater damage to the airplane and perhaps further endanger the lives of the occupants.

John raised the flaps and placed the landing gear handle in the up position. He climbed the airplane to 3,500 feet and began to circle. Dick said, "John, side slip the airplane from side to side with the wheels down and see if you can get them to lock manually." John lowered the landing gear handle once again and tried chinking the airplane from side to side as violently as he could to jar the landing gear as hard as possible. Still no lights came on.

Dick advised making one more pass directly onto the runway at just above stalling speed. He would stand just to the side of the runway one more time with a pair of binoculars and attempt to determine if the gear was locked.

The flaps were lowered to the full down position of 40 degrees. The prop was adjusted to full fine in order to develop as much power as the engine could develop. Then the airspeed was reduced to 80 MPH. The airplane stall speed is 68 MPH so this speed would not be much margin above the stalling speed.

An even longer and lower approach was made this time. The nose of the airplane was raised to a higher position than normal and more power was applied. The airspeed reduced to 70 MPH which was just above the stalling speed. The airplane was literally hanging on the propeller as it flew down the runway at about 10 feet of elevation. Just after flying over Dick's head, full power was applied, the nose of the airplane was lowered, the flaps were retracted, and the gear handle was raised. The trees on the end of the runway came up fast, and were the major concern, but the airplane picked up speed and rose well over the top of these obstacles before reaching the end of the runway.

Dick indicated the gear looked good, but it was impossible to tell whether they were locked in place or not. Dick said, "John, you will have to make a decision to land on the runway with wheels down and possibly not locked, or to land wheels up on the grass, your choice". Before doing this, Dick advised returning to a higher altitude and circling. "Let's think this situation over, one more time".

John climbed the airplane to 3,500 feet one more time, and circled in a holding pattern. Thoughts were rushing through John's head. Should the landing be made with wheels up on the grass, or with wheels down on the runway? This was a major decision and he had better not make the wrong one!

A wheels up landing on the grass would probably cause the least amount of damage to the airplane, but would be somewhat dangerous for the occupants. The procedure would be difficult, since there was a main road with a power line and fence on one end and a power line and trees on the other. An ordinary landing was not so difficult. With power on, the sink rate of the airplane could be controlled. The approach could be steep and the airspeed could be bled off quickly after rotation. The pilot could concentrate solely on controlling the landing and not be messing with opening doors, turning off fuel, turning off the electrical, killing the engine, and so forth, all at the critical time of making the landing.

The airplane cannot be landed on the grass in this manner because the airspeed must be reduced as much as possible during the approach. The sink rate would be faster, but the airspeed would be much slower. The airplane must be eased onto the grass at the lowest possible speed. If the landing was overshot, there would be no power to climb over the trees at the end of the runway and there would be no breaks to be relied upon. The landing would have to be perfect.

The door must be propped open on the approach. Just after crossing the power line and fence, the fuel shut off valve must be turned off, the electrical system must be turned off, the engine must be killed by pulling back on the fuel mixture, and the magnetos must be turned off. There was a lot to think about and to do at the most critical moment of handling the airplane for as gentle a touchdown as possible. All must be done in an attempt to keep the fuel from igniting if one of the fuel tanks was ruptured during the landing. Also, if the engine was stopped, and provided the propeller quit turning and remained in the proper position while landing, it would not hit the ground and damage both the prop and the engine.

If the airplane was landed on the runway with the gear down but not locked, the landing impact would immediately fold the gear. The airplane would slide down the runway with the prop still turning. This would damage the landing gear, lower fuselage, prop and engine. This also may well be more dangerous to the occupants than a grass landing.

Is this the time to gamble? Does John dare gamble with the lives of himself and his wife? If the gear is actually down and locked, and just didn't indicate this, the best alternative would be to land on the runway. However; landing on the grass was safer but is bound to cause some damage to the airplane. A sound and safe decision must be made!

All electrical switches could be turned off ahead of time. The engine runs on the magnetos, not the electrical system. Once the electrical system is turned off, Dick could not be talked to on the radio. This would not be a major problem since the landing would take all John's attention anyway. The door could be popped open ahead of time. That left the fuel lever to be turned off.

The fuel lever was located down low on the side of the wall, next to John's left foot. Because of this awkward position, this could not be turned off just before going over the power line. It would have to be turned off before this.

Turning off the magnetos and mixture control cut off to stop the engine would all have to be accomplished early enough to concentrate solely on controlling the landing. All must be turned off well back on the approach and a "dead stick" landing with the engine not running would have to be made.

There would be much less control of the airplane without power. Judgment would have to be exactly right to get over the power line and fence and still make a gentle landing immediately on the other side. There wouldn't be much room once over the fence before the trees would be reached.

This would all be very much harder without power.

This was not the time to gamble with people's safety. John made the decision to make a wheels-up landing on the grass. This appeared to be the safest and most sensible. The airplane would have to suffer whatever damage it would sustain. Better to damage the airplane than to damage the occupants. Dick was notified of this decision on the radio.

John began to make his letdown and make preparations to enter a long approach to the grass runway. He was about to turn off the electrical system when the radio began to crackle.

Dick's voice interrupted John's thoughts. "John, have you been working on the airplane lately?" John said, "Yes, I have been working on the interior electrical system." Dick said, "Well try that. Turn it on and then turn it off again." Reaching for the on/off rheostat switch on the instrument panel, John discovered the switch was already on and the rheostat was turned down! ---------- This must be the cause of all the grief!

The switch was turned off and the landing gear was cycled. Immediately the in-transit light came on and shortly after that, the three green lights came on! Wow! What a relief! With the rheostat switched on, and the lights turned on dim, the indicator lights were actually on, but could not be seen in the bright sunlight!

By having the interior lights on, with the rheostat turned down, the lights on the dashboard were dimmed for night vision. They were actually on, but they were unable to be seen because of the bright sunlight of the day.

With a gigantic relief this was! A normal landing was made quickly without incident. A late lunch in a nice restaurant on the ground helped to sooth John and Carol's nerves. Sometimes the smallest things can be the most important and can really raise havoc when it is not correct. Thankfully, John had clear-headed advice and was able to take time to resolve this crisis before making it much worse. Their lives could have been endangered and a good airplane could have been badly bent, all because of a very small, seemingly insignificant switch. It sure pays to have good friends with sound thinking minds.

A great lesson was learned by this experience. Even though this shook everyone to the core, the overwhelming statistics that it is safer to fly in a small airplane than it is to ride in a car can not be overlooked. After this profound scare both John and Carol continued flying for many, many hundreds of hours of pleasant enjoyable flights.

A GRANDDAUGHTER'S FLYING VISIT TO DISNEYLAND

John's granddaughter had just turned six years old and was ready to begin first grade in the fall. Before this major event in her life, John and wife Carol had planned a trip by airplane around the Western United States for her. This took place during the summer months prior to the beginning of the school year. Included was a key stop at Disneyland which was the highlight for Arianna and she was excited about flying the airplane and going to see Mickey Mouse and Donald Duck. This turned out to be one of the most delightful trips ever taken in their airplane.

John had modified a car seat and a pair of ear phones to fit his granddaughter's small stature. The car seat was strapped onto the back seat of the airplane and then she was strapped firmly into the car seat. Arianna was well secured without being too tightly restricted.

The seat was situated high enough for her to be able to see out the front of the airplane as well as out the side windows. A pair of headphones had been cut down to fit on her small head. Arianna was able to listen to all the activity on the radio and talk over the intercom to her grandparents in the front seats. She was quite comfortable in her little empire and was all ready to go to Disneyland.

During the first takeoff John heard this little voice jabbering away through the intercom. She was so excited to be flying in the airplane and leaving for Disneyland. John had to quiet her down in order to talk to Flight Control on the radio. Talking on the intercom was a real novelty to Arianna and she just loved to do it.

Five minutes or so into the flight there was no longer noise coming from the back seat. Looking around John found her sound asleep. She stayed that way until making a letdown to land for the next stop. This pattern was repeated over and over again on nearly every leg of the entire trip. Arianna loved to ride in the airplane but usually slept during the middle of most flights and woke up just as the landing was about to be made.

The first leg of the trip was from Seattle to Concord, California with an intermediate stop at Roseburg, Oregon. Total flight time was just under five hours in the air. This could have been flown nonstop by conserving fuel, but it was much to long to sit in the confines of an aircraft seat. An intermediate stop was planned at Roseburg, Oregon which was about two-hour from home base. This made a good rest stop and lunch break.

After landing at Roseburg, the FBO (fixed base operator) recommended a good restaurant within walking distance. It was just far enough away to get the kinks worked out of the legs after sitting so long and it provided a little exercise before lunch.

Having a sandwich in a restaurant was much better than the usual coke and candy bar found at most small airports. This can be one of the problems when on long trips particularly when landing at predominately small airports. There is generally limited food service. Most small airports do not have restaurants even within walking distance. An anonymous wise man once said, "The greatest single danger in aviation is starving to death".

The sandwiches and the short walk did a lot of good to refresh them all. The airplane was refueled and they were soon back in the air and on their way. Again the little voice in the back seat was heard jabbering away. Another five minutes into the flight and it became quiet again.

Next stop was Concord, California. Shortly before arriving in the area John called the Unicom station on the radio. In most airports the Unicom operator will make a telephone call for an arriving pilot to alert someone to their arrival or to arrange a taxi etc. John requested their son who lived in the area be contacted by phone and advised they were to land within half an hour. By the time John landed the airplane and taxied it to the tie down area, their family was already waiting for them in the parking lot.

The airplane was taxied right up to the parking area directly in back of the Sheraton Hotel where a reservation had been made for the night's stay. The hotel provided a room with a view of the runway and tie down area. John was even able to keep an eye on the airplane from the window of their room.

After a pleasant weekend and good visit with their son and family they all piled into the airplane and strapped themselves in one more time. This time there was a little more jabbering than usual about going to Disneyland as Arianna was aware this was the final leg going into the Los Angeles area.

The heavy traffic of Los Angeles International Airport was going to be skirted around by entering the LA basin well to the east. A landing at Fullerton was planned which was the closest airport to Disneyland. It was far enough east to be out of the LAX Class B Area (Terminal Control Area).

The weather was not as good as could have been hoped for. Clouds covered 75% of the sky most of the way. Fortunately the airplane was capable of climbing high enough to get over the top of most of the weather. Most of the flight was made by rising up to 10,500 feet. If the tops of the clouds had been higher the oxygen system would have had to be used.

When arriving within 100 miles of their destination, Los Angeles Flight Watch was called on the radio to get the latest weather information at Fullerton. Flight Watch advised, "clear skies with heavy haze in the LA basin".

There are a large number of airports and control areas in the LA area to contend with. Not being familiar with these, John had previously studied the aerial map closely in order to navigate around them without violating their airspace. The route of flight was planned to fly inland east to Palmdale and then turn south to enter the LA Basin. Once over the mountains and inside the Basin, the plan was to fly directly to Fullerton. This route allowed the jet traffic landing and taking off from LAX to be avoided as well as similar traffic at major airports throughout the LA Basin.

As Flight Service had reported, the heavy haze was so thick it was nearly like flying into light clouds. The ground and all the communities below could be seen quite clearly by looking straight down; however visibility out the front was more restricted then was comfortable. The best view was directly down from the aircraft. Visibility forward was adequate to be legal but little could be seen far ahead.

This was a good test for John's new GPS. He had programmed it to display a track directly toward Fullerton Airport and the cursor needle was centered. Centering of the needle meant they were flying directly on their intended route of flight. Ground speed and distance from the airport were being displayed as the flight progressed.

After listening to Fullerton ATIS (Automatic Transcribed Information Service), John called Fullerton Approach on the radio. The controller gave him a heading which was identical with the one reflected on the GPS. This verified the airplane was right on track and was 10 nautical miles from touchdown.

Fullerton Approach turned the airplane over to the control tower when they were five miles from touchdown. The tower frequency was dialed into the radio and John made a report, "Fullerton Tower, Cherokee 8475 Charlie with you". The tower controller immediately came back with, "75 Charlie, report two mile final for runway two four right". Since a bearing of 240 degrees was being flown, this meant the tower was guiding them to a straight in landing, rather than having them enter and fly the traffic pattern.

The GPS clicked off the decreasing distance in miles and tenths of miles. When reaching two miles from touchdown, another report was made to the Tower, "75 Charlie, two mile final". The Tower came back with, "75 Charlie, clear to land. Are you familiar with the airport?" John said, "Negative, this is our first time here, 75 Charlie". The controller said, "75 Charlie, make a left hand turn, midfield after landing to exit the runway. Careful crossing two four left. Ground point 8 will direct you from there". (Ground point 8 meant to turn the radio to 122.8 in order to talk to Ground Control.)

In preparation for landing the fuel was switched to the fullest tank, the manifold pressure was reduced to 21 inches of mercury, RPM was reduced to 2100 and the nose of the airplane was raised in order to bleed off some of the airspeed and get below 150 MPH. When below this speed, the main landing gear was lowered. Three green lights appeared on the dashboard indicating the gear was down and locked. This reduced the aircraft airspeed even more, which was now down to 125. At this speed it was possible to lower the flaps without having them damaged by the slip stream. The flaps were lowered to 5 degrees and the airplane was trimmed with the electric trim, then the flaps were lowered to 20 degrees. The airplane was trimmed again, and the flaps were finally lowered to 40 degrees. Then the airplane was trimmed a final time to place it into a constant decent toward the runway.

The airspeed was now down to 100 MPH. The propeller was adjusted to full fine, the fuel mixture control was pushed to full on, and the electric fuel pump was turned on. Fuel had already been switched from left to the right tank. The airplane was now in the landing configuration.

The nose of the airplane was raised or lowered to adjust the airspeed to a constant 90 MPH. The throttle was used to increase power to adjust the line of decent up or down, directly toward the numbers on the runway threshold.

The airplane was still a little too fast, so the nose was raised slightly to bleed off the extra 10 miles per hour to the "over the fence" speed of 90 MPH. The airplane sink rate was good and the airplane was descending straight for the numbers on the end of the runway.

One last check was made to make sure the airplane was ready for the landing. The checklist "GUMP" was used, Gas, Undercarriage, Mixture and Prop. All was in order. The airplane set down onto the runway with hardly a whisper. John sure wished all landings could be made like that one was.

Disneyland through the eyes of a young granddaughter was incredible. A collapsible stroller had been packed into the airplane. This was ideal for transporting Arianna from one event to the next. Movement across the Disneyland grounds was much faster, and Arianna didn't get too tired by the end of the day. It was a little different for Grandpa John. He got a little played out.

After two days at Disneyland and one day at Knott's Berry Farm, adequate enjoyment of the theme parks was had and all were ready to travel on to the next excitement.

Next stop Lake Havasu, Arizona.

FLIGHT FROM DISNEYLAND TO HAVASU WITH THEIR GRANDAUGHTER

John, Carol and their granddaughter Arianna continued their flight in their Piper Cherokee Arrow shortly after their visit to Disneyland and Knott's Berry Farm in Anaheim. They flew from Fullerton, which was the closest airport to the theme parks and had three exciting days pushing Arianna from one exhibit to the other in her stroller.

All the bags had been loaded into the airplane including the handiest carryon of all, their granddaughter's stroller. Using this to travel from one end of Disneyland and Knott's Berry Farm to the other had been a terrific help.

Arianna was strapped into the car seat in one of the back seats one more time and her specially modified ear phones were placed over her ears. She was very proud of her little perch on her private throne in the back of the airplane. John and Carol piled into the airplane and they were all soon airborne and headed out of the Los Angeles Basin toward Lake Havasu, Arizona.

Arianna watched out the window for an exceptionally long time at all the activity passing by on the ground. There were several communities passed over. The airplane route of flight was adjacent to a number of large airports. There flight was well out of the traffic pattern, but many airplanes were seen taking off and landing.

This kept Arianna quite busy and her jabbering over the intercom continued for longer than normal. When flying over the hills surrounding the Los Angeles Basin, all became quiet again and a quick glance to the back seat verified Arianna had fallen asleep one more time. She had done this on every leg of the trip so far.

Next stop was Lake Havasu, Arizona. From Fullerton to Lake Havasu is a little over an hour's flight. It is only 180 air miles so this is one of the shorter legs of their entire trip.

The hospitality shown by the airport personnel on all stops had been outstanding, but this one was exceptional. Upon landing and tying down the airplane at the new airport at Lake Havasu, John's party was met by the airport manager. He drove a jitney with a trailer attached to it right to their airplane and helped with the unloading of all the baggage. All piled onto the jitney, including Arianna on top of several bags on the trailer, and were driven to the FBO office.

The FBO suggested a motel that would come to the airport and to pick them up and take them to the motel, free of charge! This was unusually convenient and saved renting a car. The motel was within walking distance of the London Bridge and offered rooms at 50% off to airplane pilots. It seemed the manager of the motel was also a pilot. The FBO and motel manager couldn't have been more accommodating and their efforts were certainly appreciated.

The motel van picked them up within 15 minutes of John's call and took them to the motel. They were given a spacious double room overlooking Lake Havasu with a magnificent view of the London Bridge.

The London Bridge is situated between the mainland and an island close to the shore of Lake Havasu. This is a spectacular sight and pleasant to view from the motel window.

The ancient bridge which, as the children's song describes had been falling down for several hundred years. This was uprooted from the streets of London, torn down and shipped to Havasu piece by piece, and then reconstructed on this new location.

What a feat this had been to dismantle this bridge block by block, number all the blocks and transport the pieces all the way from England and then reconstruct them here in Havasu.

Dismantling the bridge and reconstructing it piece by piece was just short of a modern day miracle. Each rock block had been coded with its location by numbering as it was removed. Reconstruction was accomplished by using these numbers. The reconstruction contractor was able to locate the original architectural drawings for the bridge. These had been used during the original construction 600 years previously. The plans were reused for the reconstruction and were reported as being extremely useful.

After a quick rest in the motel, the stroller was unfolded for Arianna to sit in and she rode in her little chariot a few blocks down the street to the London Bridge area. Many souvenir shops were along the walkway under the bridge which were interesting to browse through.

The weather couldn't have been more beautiful. It was 80 degrees and the desert humidity was extremely low. How much more ideal than this could it get? Their stroll along the lake on one side of their walkway and all the shops on the other side was very pleasant.

People began to gather under one of the arches of the bridge in the evening. Folding chairs had been brought along and all began to sit facing a stage under the bridge at one end of the first arch. John, Carol and Arianna decided to find out what the excitement was all about.

A few tables and chairs were available for those who didn't have folding chairs. John and Carol were lucky enough to find one of these with enough room left for the three of them

After a few minutes of sitting there waiting for something to happen, an orchestra entered the stage and began playing music. The large number of people who had gathered carrying their folding chairs could hardly be believed. John and Carol estimated the number of people sitting under the large arch, listening to the music, to be more than 1,000.

It was such a pleasant evening, with the temperature ideal and the entertainment so outstanding, they sat there until nearly 10:00 PM. Their stomachs told them it was way past time to eat and they had better find something soon. Fortunately there was a restaurant nearby that was still serving dinner at that time of the evening.

The next day was spent browsing around the shops under the London Bridge. There was another concert that evening as well under the arch of the bridge. John's party arrived early enough to capture the same seats they had used the night before. This turned out to be another great way to spend an evening. Along with the music, there were a number of entertaining skits and even a square dance troop. An entertaining free show was really enjoyed. Their stay in Havasu was so pleasant they hated to leave. Even their granddaughter had a great time and nearly didn't want to leave. The next destination however was the Grand Canyon and even though Arianna didn't quite know what the Grand Canyon was, the thought of riding in the airplane and seeing something else new was enough to convince her they should be moving on.

Shortly after breakfast the motel van picked them up with all their bags and headed for the airport. It was already 80 degrees so the takeoff run was going to be a little longer than usual.

The manager of the airport met their van with the jitney and trailer, picked up their bags and headed for the airplane. What hospitality! They were fueled and loaded in short order and quickly moved down the runway on their way to the next destination, the fabulous Grand Canyon.

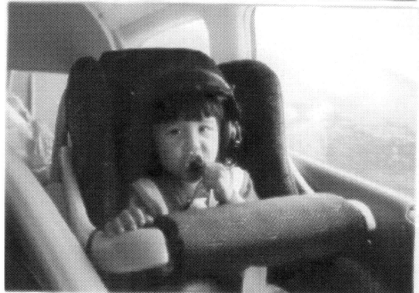

GRANDDAUGHTER ARIANNA ON THE WAY TO
DISNEYLAND ARIANNA PROVIDING INSTRUCTIONS TO
THE PILOT

ARRIVING AT FULLERTON, CA. – NEXT STOP
DISNEYLAND
THE MISPLACED LONDON BRIDGE

FLIGHT TO THE GRAND CANYON WITH THEIR GRANDAUGHTER

The next one-hour leg of their trip took them to Grand Canyon Airport on the southern rim of the Canyon. This airport is 6606 feet high and is the highest airport John had ever made a landing at. Landing and taking off was anticipated to be a different experience because of the high altitude and thin air.

Flying at 9,500 feet elevation, the Grand Canyon Airport could be seen from a great distance away. Normally a runway can only be seen when within 5 or 6 miles from an airport. Many times the runway cannot be seen at all until arriving right on top of it. From that altitude flying in the clean dry air, the runway could be seen at Grand Canyon Airport during their approach, more than 25 miles away. Even from this distance the long cut made through the trees was unusually distinctive.

The control tower directed John to enter the pattern for the left runway. The airport being more than a mile high, John felt there would be a multitude of differences landing there. It was bound to be different from landing at his home airport which was just above sea level.

The only major difference John actually noticed was that a lot more power had to be used to hold the right altitude on landing. Also more power had to be used to maintain the "over the fence" air speed of 90 MPH. All else seemed much the same and one of his more "whisper landings" was made. (In this instance whisper means a quiet landing, not John's usual statement, "be quiet about my landings".)

A car was rented to drive to the Grand Canyon South entrance. The view from the car was restricted by bushes along the side of the road. The Canyon had not been seen while driving to the first viewing area. Arianna got out of the car and walked down the path in front of them. As she walked to the rim and caught the first glimpse of the Canyon all that could be heard was, "Oh, My God!" This just about says it all. The beauty and grandeur of the Grand Canyon defies all description.

The wind was blowing quite hard the day of the scheduled departure, so an extra day sightseeing at the Canyon was spent. If a flight had been attempted that day over the Canyon in such a high wind it would have been quite bumpy and no one would have enjoyed the ride very much.

Next day the wind had died down and the weather was beautiful. It had been a good decision to delay the flight. The next leg of the trip was to be over the canyon for about 150 miles, and then on into Las Vegas.

When reviewing the weight and balance of the airplane to calculate takeoff performance, John determined the high altitude and heat of the day would require much more runway than usual. Breakfast was to be early in order to get airborne during the coolest part of the morning when more lift was available. Breakfast was at 6:00 AM. The airplane was loaded, fueled and ready to go by 7:30. This must have set some sort of a record, as it normally took two hours or so just to get ready for breakfast.

While running up the engine for the magneto check and to cycle hot oil into the propeller's variable pitch mechanism, an extra function was added to the checklist. John revved up the engine and leaned the fuel flow from full on to obtain the maximum power when the engine was at full throttle during the actual takeoff.

All high altitude airports are a problem for non-supercharged reciprocating engines as is in the Cherokee. The air is much thinner, therefore when the engine is revved to its maximum for takeoff, it requires less fuel and more air. If the fuel is not leaned, the mixture will be too rich and the engine will not reach peak horsepower just when it is needed the most. In this event the airplane would require an even greater distance for takeoff.

After running through the complete checklist, the engine was revved to its maximum and the fuel mixture was leaned to the point the engine was running at its peak. By adjusting the fuel mixture, the EGT (exhaust gas temperature) was slightly backed off from peak temperature by increasing the fuel flow slightly. Leaving the fuel mixture lever at this setting the engine RPM was lowered to a fast idle and preparation was made for the takeoff.

The checklist was complete and the fuel mixture was now set for peak performance at this high altitude airport. This left only one more item that would help John's takeoff from the high altitude. The flaps were lowered to 5 degrees, which was the first notch, to create additional lift. Lowering the flaps beyond this point would create a great deal more drag, which would offset the gain of the added lift.

John's granddaughter had been strapped into her private seat in the back and had placed her specially made head phones over her ears. She was chattering away into the intercom as usual. Once in the air she didn't go to sleep as she normally would have. The view out the window over the Grand Canyon was so spectacular she wasn't about to go to sleep on this entire leg.

Flight over the Grand Canyon was made at 2000 feet above the rim. Restrictions apply to flights into the Canyon any lower than this. Monitoring a certain frequency on the radio was also required. It was interesting for all of them to listen to this frequency as the tour aircraft could be heard reporting their positions every so many minutes. It was possible to locate their position and each aircraft could be followed on the aerial map.

Pictures were taken with the video camera out the windows. John's granddaughter was impressed with the spectacular view below which kept her awake and occupied during most of this flight.

Soon after taking off from the Grand Canyon Airport, a very perplexing incident happened. After a few minutes in the air the retractable landing gear system in the Piper Cherokee Arrow began to act in a very strange manner. The air speed suddenly lowered from the normal cruise speed to 20 MPH slower than normal. Oh oh, what was this all about? John hurriedly scanned the instrument panel looking for anything out of the ordinary.

Wow! The three green landing gear lights were on! This indicated the landing gear was down and locked and this should not have been the case. The gear had just been raised during take off and John had not taken any action to lower it!

Further review of the instruments revealed the gear handle was still in the up position, not down! Somehow the gear had to have dropped on its own, without being activated! What was this all about?

John quickly lowered the gear handle and then raised it again. The gear cycled and came up and locked into the wing of the airplane. All seemed to be normal. What in the world would cause the landing gear to drop, once it had been raised, without the landing gear retract control handle being touched? This was a complete mystery, but all seemed to be in order with the system now. At least the landing gear was staying up in place where it belonged.

John continued the flight while scratching his head trying to determine what possibly could have caused this malfunction.

The landing at Henderson Airport, near Las Vegas was anticipated in the extreme heat of the late summer afternoon. This airport was located about 10 miles south of the Las Vegas Strip and the temperature outside the airplane at cruise altitude of 8,500 feet had already risen to 90 degrees. This meant the temperature on the ground could be anticipated to be more than 100 degrees. This was extremely hot for landing on a relatively high altitude airport.

Lake Mead came into view after an hour's flight. This is the water in the reservoir behind Boulder Dam. A number of houseboats were seen lumbering along in the reservoir and people waved as the airplane flew by.

Once flying over the water, John made a turn to the northwest to be able to fly over Boulder Dam. Soon the dam came into view. Two slow steep turns were made directly over the face of the dam in order to look down and get the best view. Cars were driving across the top and people were seen walking on the sidewalk. Several people standing on the top of the dam were waving as the airplane passed over their head.

Henderson Field outside Las Vegas was just a short distance away.

FLIGHT TO LAS VEGAS

They soon flew out of the mountains surrounding Lake Mead and the giant structure of Boulder Dam and were headed for Henderson Airport located in the southern suburbs of Las Vegas. Their granddaughter was sitting on her little throne in the back seat with her modified ear phones over her ears. She had not slept on this leg of their journey as the trip over the Grand Canyon and Lake Mead had been so spectacular. Her little voice could be heard over the intercom jabbering away.

While approaching the vicinity of the Henderson Airport, all was going smoothly until suddenly a slight bump was felt and a dull thud was heard. What in the world was that? Had the airplane hit a bird, or had something else caused this? John hurriedly scanned the instruments once more and the air speed was found to have dropped once again! He was confounded to discover that the three green lights for the landing gear were lit again, indicating the gear had dropped a second time!

John found the gear handle was still in the up position, but the gear had come down once again without being activated. He lowered the gear handle and then raised it again. The gear came up and locked into place and the green lights went out. All seemed normal. This was very perplexing. What would cause the gear to go down by itself? Henderson field was only a short way away and John would have the gear system checked there. He lowered the wheels and left them down until the landing was made.

Henderson Field was just a few minutes away and another whisper landing was soon made there. The temperature had already risen to over 100 degrees. It was a bit hot renting their rental car and unloading the baggage for their stay in Las Vegas.

An aircraft mechanic was available on the field and John asked him to have a look at the airplane and possibly fix anything that might be wrong with the gear actuating system.

The licensed aircraft mechanic on duty went over the entire landing gear system thoroughly. The airplane was raised onto wing jacks and the gear was cycled several times. Nothing could be found to be wrong with the entire system. This was not only perplexing, but was the source of a great uneasy feeling for John to continue the flight on home.

John rented a car at the airport and drove them all a short way into Las Vegas to visit some of their friends. All the time John still pondered why this gear problem had repeated itself. Why the cause of this couldn't be found was a complete mystery. He gave serious thought to the advisability of flying on home with this problem not being resolved. On the other hand a competent aircraft mechanic had gone over the entire retract system and had found nothing wrong. John concluded there just wasn't anything more that could be done so they would go on, but this had become a major concern in his mind. Any danger involved would have to be seriously considered.

They took their granddaughter to the Circus Circus casino and hotel. She was able to watch the circus acts while John and Carol checked into the hotel. The hotel also had an indoor amusement park, complete with rollercoaster. This was definitely not John and Carol's cup of tea but their granddaughter enjoyed several of the less sever rides and grandpa had to accompany her.

They took their granddaughter to their favorite casino, which was Caesar's Palace. This has a large shopping mall with clouds and blue sky painted on the ceiling. Walking down below, looking up at the ceiling, makes the clouds seem to move along in the direction they were walking. By turning around and walking in the opposite direction the clouds seemed to move in the opposite direction.

Once every so many minutes, the statues in the courtyard seemingly come to life and started to move and talk. This was really impressive to their granddaughter and it startled the daylight out of her when they first sprang to life.

Next day the temperature in Las Vegas rose to 110 degrees. Had it not been so dry, this would have been nearly unbearable. The swimming pool at their friend's home had become the coolest place in town and many relaxing hours were spent living up the "Good Life", relaxing and soaking up the magnificent sunshine. Even for her young age, Arianna had become a powerful swimmer and spent most of the day in the pool. A few days of this really thawed out their bones after the long wet winter experienced in the Seattle area.

Las Vegas was a great place to visit even with the little kids like their granddaughter. She had a great time. Gambling held no interest for John and Carol, but walking through the huge newer casinos was most enjoyable. Sometimes a quarter or two was put into the slot machines, but mostly just a walk was made through the casino to enjoy the décor and to watch the people.

The landing gear problem haunted John's thoughts throughout their entire stay in Las Vegas. What could have caused the gear to drop? Low hydraulic oil pressure could possibly cause this. No, that couldn't be, this was checked. All the hydraulic hoses were also checked for leaks and none were found. If something major was wrong, why would the gear drop intermittently and not all the time? A possible solution just could not be found.

There were two more major legs remaining to be flown to get home. This condition was a great concern, but there was no purpose served in having another mechanic look at the airplane. One had already looked at the entire system and had thoroughly gone through everything. He had pronounced the system to have a clean bill of health, with no abnormalities. It was only a four hour trip to the next destination. Even if the gear did come down again, it was not a dangerous threat. The airplane could be flown with the gear down, if necessary. This problem would have to be left alone for now—unless it happened again

LAS VEGAS TO SEATTLE

The departure from Henderson was not the usual takeoff and climb because of the effect of the heat of the day. This coupled with the relatively high altitude airport and the near maximum gross weight of the airplane made the climb out of the Las Vegas Basin a hard struggle.

John, Carol and granddaughter had decided to leave early in the morning when the air temperature would be at its coolest. By the time breakfast was over, the rental car had been checked in and the airplane had been fueled and loaded, the air temperature had already risen to 100 degrees.

With full fuel tanks and lots of baggage, the airplane was already heavy and near the maximum takeoff weight. The takeoff run was extra long because of the lack of lift caused by these adverse factors. The runway was a mile long and most of it was used to get off the ground to become airborne.

Once under way, John suspected the gear drop system might still give them trouble. This was still weighing heavily on his mind.

The automatic gear drop system was programmed to lower the gear when the airplane slowed below 110 MPH. Just in case this system was still malfunctioning, John made a decision to leave the landing gear extended well after takeoff.

The normal liftoff speed of 70 MPH was increased to 80 MPH prior to rotation. Even then the airplane left the ground sluggishly and began to climb slowly because of the heat and high elevation.

The landing gear was kept down as planned until the airplane was well into the air. The airspeed was allowed to increase to 120 MPH before the gear was raised. The gear cycled normally and did not drop back down, as John halfway expected it to do.

Shortly after departure on this extremely hot day, a fantastic event was about to be experienced. All three factors of heat, high altitude and heavy gross weight were fighting against the airplane's ability to climb into the air. Every foot of altitude gained seemed to be a struggle. John was about to get some help from the wind.

The TCA (Terminal Control Area, currently known as Class B Area) had to be flown under until nearly to the mountains surrounding the western side of the Las Vegas Valley. They could not enter the Class B area without permission as they were flying visually (VFR).

Once out from under the Class B Area, John had to climb abruptly in order to reach altitude adequate to clear the mountain range. This meant staying below 5,000 feet until nearly to the base of the mountains, and then having to climb to 7,500 feet in order to go over the lowest part of the mountain ridge.

The temperature was 105 degrees at takeoff and was still above 90 degrees when the airplane reached 4,500 feet. The climb to cruise altitude was progressing slowly.

Gaining enough altitude was taking forever. The hot air and high altitude of the terrain was providing little lift, and the airplane just didn't want to climb. Fortunately, there was a tail wind of 25 knots, and this was about to give the struggle a helping hand.

As the nose of the airplane was raised, the airspeed reduced to the climbing speed of 100 MPH. A half-mile of altitude was going to have to be gained to get high enough to clear the mountains. The airplane climb was extremely slow, as expected. It seemed to take forever to even get half way up the mountain. Enough altitude could not be gained by the time the mountains were reached, so it was necessary for John to begin a slow circle.

The mountains began to fill the forward view of the windshield each time the airplane came closer. John continued to hold the bank into a large, slow circle. He was gaining altitude at an extremely slow rate but each time he came closer to the mountain the airplane began to climb much faster.

John flew the airplane in circle after circle. Not much room was available to maneuver. The mountains were on one side and the Class B Area was on the other. The Class B Area could not be entered without violating the rules unless John requested permission to enter. He didn't want to do this so the slow circles couldn't be as large as he would have liked them to have been.

John found the wind currents along side the mountain were beginning to be an aid. Every time he went near the mountain face the airplane began to climb much faster. He pointed the nose of the airplane directly toward the face of the mountain and flew even closer. It began to pickup lift.

John edged even closer to the face of the mountain and then turned parallel to it. His maneuvering began to work. He had found the strongest part of the rising air current. The airplane began to rise much more rapidly.

This is called "slope soaring" and is one of the methods glider pilots use to gain altitude without power. The wind blowing against the side of the mountain is being forced up, causing a strong updraft. This can be a real advantage to help an airplane gain altitude.

This time it began to work better than it ever had for John. It was amazing just how powerful the wind was to be able to pick up a one and one half ton fully loaded airplane and raise it nearly effortlessly into the air.

The wind was quite powerful and the airplane began to climb at an extremely rapid rate. The more the climb rate increased, the more John pulled the control column back and the higher the nose of the airplane was raised. The airspeed began to reduce but the airplane began to rise very fast.

The air current began taking the airplane up at the phenomenal rate of 1,500 feet per minute. This was twice the normal climb rate with just engine power under normal conditions at this altitude.

After a few minutes of flying in this rising air, the climb rate increased to a phenomenal 2000 feet per minute. John pulled the control column back even further and the nose of the airplane was raised even higher.

The airplane began to go up like an elevator at top speed. The lift increased even greater, to 2,500 feet per minute. This was more than three times normal! The pitch of the airplane was increased again to an extremely nose high attitude. The climb continued at this fast rate for several minutes. In the mean time the airspeed forward of the airplane had reducing even more. A phenomenal thing began to happen. The airplane was being lifted by the strong updraft but the extreme nose high attitude of the airplane wasn't allowing it to fly forward.

Suddenly, the stall warning buzzer began to buzz in their headphones. The nose of the airplane had been held so steep the airplane was no longer flying forward, just up! It was actually in a stall, and yet it was still going up at a fantastic rate! The rising air current was lifting the airplane at the phenomenal rate of 2,500 feet per minute, but the airplane was not flying forward, and was actually suspended like a feather in the wind.

John lowered the nose of the airplane just enough to allow it to be flying forward and not in a stall. This just above stall condition was held by John for a long time by keeping the nose of the airplane high. The airplane continued to go up, up, up!

What a strange feeling! It was as if the airplane was standing still and yet was being lifted by the exceptionally strong up draft. Moments went by and the airplane continued to rise like a cork in a bottle of water. Little time was taken to reach the top of the ridge.

When the necessary altitude to get over the ridge was gained, John lowered the nose and the airplane began to gain airspeed forward once more. The desert area on the other side of the ridge could be seen as the airplane become level and had come up to cruising speed. John banked toward their destination. As suddenly as they had flown into the strong rising air current, they flew out of it. The air became much smoother and the airplane was once again flying normally.

This maneuver had taken less than one quarter of the usual time it would normally take to climb over the mountains in this extreme heat. They were over the ridge and on their way out of the Las Vegas Basin in a much shorter time than it would have taken without the help of the wind.

What an experience this had been! It was understandable why glider pilots become hooked on their sport. This was an unusual event for a powered airplane and had been a real thrill to have experienced.

It was amazing how a ton and a half airplane, loaded with three people, full fuel tanks, and lots of baggage could be lifted at this phenomenal rate by just the power of the wind. Once over the ridge their route of flight was down a large flat valley adjacent to Death Valley toward their next destination. Next stop was Carson City. Generally when flying to the Reno area their destination had been the Reno-Stead airport. During this trip, the Reno Air Races were being held and the airport was closed to transient traffic. Cannon Airport, in the center of Reno, is always extra busy with jet traffic, and tie downs for the airplane are expensive there. Carson City Airport was chosen as their next stop since little traffic is being experienced and the tie downs are free.

The airplane was landed and refueled and a courtesy car was borrowed to use to take them to a motel for the night. The last leg of their trip was coming up.

The departure from Carson City the next morning was made shortly after breakfast. This would be a flight from Carson City back to their home airport near Seattle, with a rest stop in Bend, Oregon. Total flying time would be four hours.

The problem being experienced with the landing gear extending was still much in John's mind and the takeoff procedure of leaving the gear down until a higher speed was obtained was used. Once airborne and up to adequate speed, John raised the landing gear. No difficulty was experienced. Fortunately the landing gear problem did not resurface all the way back to their home base.

Their granddaughter slept most of the way, as usual. A landing at Crest Airpark near Seattle brought to a close their most enjoyable trip to Concord, California, Disneyland, Lake Havasu, Grand Canyon, Las Vegas and Reno. They had a number of exciting experiences, particularly their granddaughter, but all were glad to be home. Their travels had taken them 2,300 air miles with 16 hours of airborne time flown on the airplane.

THE AUTOMATIC GEAR DROP SYSTEM

The weather turned bad for flying shortly after arriving home. The Seattle area can sometimes do this. The airplane sat in the hanger for nearly a month before another flight was made. Eventually the sun came out and flying conditions improved. It was time to go flying again.

All during the period of bad weather the problem experienced with the landing gear extension had weighed heavily on John's mind. It was strongly suspected there might be additional trouble brewing. He wasn't wrong!

The airplane is equipped with an automatic landing gear system. It is designed to automatically lower the landing gear when the airplane slows to below 110 MPH. It is a safety system designed to keep from landing the airplane without the gear extended, which would ruin everyone's total day.

This system operated from a pressure/vacuum pitot tube. The pitot tube for this is located just outside the pilot's window, on the left side of the airplane. When not flying the airplane, this pitot tube normally has a cover placed over it so foreign objects like bees etc. can not climb into it. For some reason this pitot tube cover had inadvertently been left off during the time the airplane had been on the ground. This factor played a large part in the problem of the gear rising and lowering by itself.

The pitot tube has two holes in it. Each hole is connected to a hose. One hole faces forward. This catches the air and creates pressure into the tube. The other hole faces sideways to the air stream. The air passing this creates a vacuum. One hole and tube has pressure and the other hole and tube has vacuum.

The other ends of the connecting hoses are connected to a small vacuum chamber. The center of the chamber has a rubber bladder in it, which divides the chamber into two sides. The pressure hose is connected to one side and the vacuum hose is connected to the other side.

During the time the airplane is flying above 110 miles per hour, the action of the pressure and vacuum moves the rubber diaphragm toward the vacuum side. When the airplane slows below 110 MPH the pressure and vacuum both decrease. This allows the bladder to move to the pressure side.

This movement of the bladder activates the landing gear system. The system is designed so that it will be nearly impossible to land with the wheels up. This sounds complicated but actually the system is well engineered and operates quite efficiently.

The gear problem had nearly been forgotten as a short hop around the traffic pattern was being made to warm up the engine so John could change the oil.

Takeoff was normal and the gear was raised. The gear immediately went down! The speed of the airplane was raised to 120 MPH and the gear was raised again. It went down again! The same thing happened over and over, several times. The gear would just not stay up. Every time it was raised, it would immediately go back down.

The air speed was kept below 150 MPH in order to keep the landing gear doors from being damaged. The slip stream above this speed could severely damage them. John throttled back and headed for Harvey Field, 30 miles away. A good mechanic was located there, and it looked as if he had better have a look at the entire landing gear system.

There is also a hand operated emergency system in the airplane for raising and lowering the landing gear should the regular system fail. This consists of a lever between the two front seats. When the lever is raised, the gear will raise. Pushing down on the lever will result in the gear being lowered.

The regular gear handle was left in the up position and the gear was raised using the emergency lever. The gear came up and stayed in the up position – provided John kept his finger lifting up on the emergency gear lever.

When John reached Harvey Field, he released the emergency lever and the gear went down. The regular gear handle was also lowered to the down position. It would be dangerous to have the gear suddenly come back up, just as the airplane was about to touch down on the runway. The gear stayed down during the landing.

What in the world would cause this system to completely malfunction after the airplane had sat for nearly a month? What had changed during this time? It worked properly during the last part of their long trip, but it didn't work at all now. Why? What had changed in the interim? This was a complete puzzlement.

The mechanic was busy with other aircraft when John arrived. He recommended the airplane be flown back to Crest leaving the gear down and to come back in the middle of next week when he had time to work on it.

The flight back to Crest Airpark with the wheels down was slow. Once on the ground, the rear seats and the floorboards were removed in preparation for the mechanic to work on the emergency gear drop system the next week. It seemed logical the problem was with the emergency gear activation system itself.

John removed the floor boards and had a good look. There appeared to be nothing visibly wrong with the vacuum chamber and activation mechanism. Everything appeared in good working order.

John thought perhaps one of the hoses leading from the pitot tube to the vacuum chamber had become plugged. This was the only thing he could think of that could cause the system to act as it had. The hoses were taken off at the vacuum chamber end. Nothing was wrong here.

The opposite end of the hoses were removed from the pitot tube and checked by shoving a wire into the pitot tube. When the wire was removed a small amount of foreign material came out on the end of it. Then a bee came crawling out of the opening! The tube was completely closed with bee's wax! The foreign material lodged in it was about four inches long and had completely blocked one tube.

The entire problem had been caused by a bee climbing inside the pitot tube and making a nest of bees wax. This says a great deal for not forgetting to cover the pitot tube when the airplane is on the ground!

The pressure and vacuum hoses were both removed and given a good cleaning. The system was put back together and has worked well ever since! The problem was solved and even better, a major maintenance bill had been avoided.

JUST PLANE EXCITMENT

Perhaps the most exciting trip of John's entire life in an airplane was generated through a series of somewhat bizarre events. For a long period of time, the weather had been poor for flying. The Seattle area had nothing but overcast skies and drizzly rain for days during September and October. It seemed as if a few good days would never arrive. A trip to Montana had been on hold for what seemed an eternity.

The weather cleared abruptly and Flight Service indicated it was to continue that way for several days, or so the forecasters predicted. John hurriedly organized a flight for a few days before Thanksgiving, with a return flight back to Seattle in time for turkey dinner with the family.

The Piper Cherokee Arrow, waiting patiently in the hanger, glistened as it was rolled into the sunshine. The engine was fired up, and the trip over three mountain ranges of western Washington, Idaho and Montana was about to begin.

Bright sunshine and clear skies, with the prevailing wind heading in the same direction, allowed for a comfortable and relatively uneventful flight. The 40 knot tail wind at altitude pushed the airplane to a constant ground speed in excess of 200 MPH, nearly all the way. It didn't take long to get there. The return trip was going to turn out to be something considerably different.

While circling the small city in Montana upon arrival, the usual pre-landing ritual was performed by cycling the propeller several times. This made one heck of a racket and usually alerted everyone in the neighborhood to the fact that a strange airplane had arrived on the scene and was about to land at the airport.

Once the arrival was announced, the race to the airport was on. One of John's brothers usually heard this and then tried to get to the airport in his car before the airplane could be landed and tied down. He usually won. This time wasn't any different. His car arrived before the wheels of the airplane touched the ground.

A few days later the weather turned cold, as it often does in northern Montana this time of year. The temperature dropped from 60 degrees above, to 10 degrees below zero overnight.

There is an old saying concerning seasons in Montana, "spring lasts about two days between winter and summer, and then summer lasts only one week. The rest is winter."

This weather change was making a disaster of plans for John to fly back home. Protecting the airplane while on the ground at the airport was beginning to be a major problem. The airplane was completely unprotected from the intense cold and strong wind as it was tied down out on the open apron.

The local airport had several small hangers available, so arrangements were hurriedly made to rent one of these. Plans for getting home for Thanksgiving were rapidly unraveling.

John's attempt to move the airplane into the hanger was thwarted by the size of the hanger. The airplane wouldn't fit inside! The fin and rudder were too high and too wide and would not allow the airplane to go all the way in to this small hanger. Undaunted by this, John turned the airplane around and shoved it in nose first as far as it would go. The doors were closed against the fuselage as tightly as they could be, leaving the fin, rudder and elevators remaining outside. This would help a great deal, but was not the best, as the hanger could not be heated with the doors halfway open. At least the engine and forward part of the airplane were somewhat protected from the savage wind and intense cold.

During the night it began to snow and the wind began to blow even harder. By morning there was 12 inches of new snow on the ground, and the temperature had dropped to minus 15 degrees below zero. The strong wind blew a four-foot snowdrift behind the airplane.

It was beginning to look as if flying was going to be impossible for the duration of the winter. Thanksgiving dinner at home looked highly unlikely, and the family was going to be greatly disappointed. The temperature remained near minus 15 degrees during the next few nights and only warmed to around 10 above during the days. It became obvious something more would have to be done to keep the engine of the airplane from getting completely cold soaked. If the oil became congealed from the intense cold, the engine undoubtedly would not start, and a trip home would be completely out of the question.

An electric light chord was rigged with a 100-watt light bulb. This was placed directly under the engine, which would allow the heat from the bulb to keep the engine oil at least partially warm. A large piece of insulation was placed over the upper cowling to help retain the heat from the light bulb. This was the best that could be done for the moment.

The next few days remained bitterly cold. The prospect for making it home for Thanksgiving was almost gone. The old "get there itis" was still very strong, but hope of making it home for Thanksgiving dinner was fading rapidly.

Several days later the sun emerged from the cold white frozen mist for the first time. It was still very cold, but the first flyable day had finally arrived after 10 days of intense cold and foul weather. John's suitcases were hurriedly thrown into the car, and a trip to the airport was made in record time.

The four-foot snowdrift behind the airplane had to be dealt with first. Three paths had to be shoveled to make a trail for the nose and main landing gear. After nearly an hour of exhaustive exertion, with snow flying in all directions, it was finally possible to move the airplane out of the hanger to a location where the engine could be started.

John jumped into the airplane and made ready for the start. He first attempted to move the engine controls to the starting position. The fuel mixture was frozen solid and couldn't be moved. The throttle was also frozen, but with a little persuasion it was possible to move these just enough to allow the engine to start. If the engine could be started, the warmth from the engine running would soon thaw everything else. Fortunately, the 100-watt light bulb had done its job and had kept the oil warm enough to circulate once the engine started.

Pressure was strong for John to make this trip today, rather than wait any longer. The weather in northern Montana was, at best, unpredictable and the clear skies could change in a heart beat. It was either go now or possible remain stuck for several more days.

A quick call to Flight Service indicated strong winds aloft with clearing skies to the west. Since west was the direction of John's flight, this seemed to be a reasonably good forecast, and a "go" decision was made. This turned out to be not one of his better decisions. Little heed had been taken of the forecasted upper winds and it was not foreseen just how strong those winds were going to become.

Surprisingly, the engine started with the third turn over. While it was running and warming up, tracks were made on the runway by driving the car back and forth to pack the snow down. A series of small snowdrifts had to be driven over several times.

The snow was still quite soft and would hold the airplane back from gaining takeoff speed. John planned to make a soft field takeoff but neglected to tell his brother that he was going to do this. This maneuver would allow the airplane to become airborne as quickly as possible to get clear of the soft snow that would be holding the acceleration back. Once leaving the snow covered ground the airplane, while still in "ground effect" would pickup flying speed much more rapidly. To the uninitiated, this maneuver can be startling.

Communication was going to be accomplished through use of a hand held radio with John's brother on the ground. The range of his radio was quite short when transmitting, so contact could continue only during the first 25 miles or so of the flight.

The airplane was taxied over the trail prepared for it through the snow to the end of the runway. A miniature blizzard was created in back of the airplane. The checklist was thoroughly gone through to make doubly sure that everything was in order. The engine oil was now in its proper heat range and the cylinder head temperature was reading normal. The checklist was complete, and all was in readiness.

John lined up the airplane onto the landing strip and pushed the throttle to the firewall while the brakes were being held and the fuel mixture was adjusted. The engine revved to its peak for this moderately high elevation while a small adjustment was made to the fuel mixture. A soft field takeoff was about to be made, which could be startling if not prepared to be witnessed.

The flaps were lowered to 20 degrees, the brakes were released and the control column was pulled all the way back into John's lap immediately. The airplane surged ahead. The wheels could be felt hitting the small snowdrifts as the airplane jerked down the runway being held back somewhat by the soft snow. The air speed quickly built to about 50 MPH, and because the control column was pulled all the way back, the airplane leaped into the air. It was airborne, but was not ready to fly. It was not going fast enough. Ground effect was the only thing keeping the airplane in the air at all. The airspeed was still too low for normal flight.

The landing gear and flaps were quickly raised and the airplane was pointed slightly down to just below the level position. John held it there until the speed built to 80 MPH. The nose of the airplane was gently raised while the airspeed built to 100 and the airplane began to rise into the air. The airplane was leveled and held there until the airspeed built to the normal cruising speed. The grand odyssey was about to begin.

In the hurry to get under way John had neglected to inform his brother that he was going to make a soft field takeoff. When the airplane rose off the runway, after having gone only a short distance with the airspeed obviously inadequate for takeoff, it appeared as if something had gone terribly wrong. The airplane sank toward the ground as the landing gear and flaps were raised. The airplane appeared destined to crash. A soft field take off hadn't been witnessed for years, and no preparation had been made to witness this one. All went well though, which ended the moment of terror.

A frantic radio call was made from the ground with a very concerned voice on the other end saying, "Don't do that again without advising me first! You scared the hell out of me!"

The first mountain range on the route of flight was about 60 miles away. Once the cruise airspeed of 150 MPH had been reached, the airplane was pointed at the sky and the long climb began. Altitude had to be gained from around 4,000 feet to 9,500 feet or more, for the airplane to clear the mountains.

At 9000 feet, a fierce weather front could be seen moving in fast from the west. John was heading right for it. If this flight was to continue, it would have to be over the top of this, or the race back to the airport would be on.

The top of the clouds appeared high. It remained to be seen whether the airplane could climb high enough to get over the top of the on coming storm, or whether it would be necessary to turn around and return to the airport. If that was necessary John may very well be having to land in a snow storm.

The portable oxygen bottle mounted in the back seat was turned on. The breathing mask was put in place and the system was adjusted for altitude shortly after reaching 11,000 feet. At 14,500, which is the theoretical absolute ceiling for this airplane, the top of the overcast still had not been reached. It was questionable whether the airplane could climb high enough to get over this cloudbank.

John's brother called from the ground to advise the storm was coming in fast, and that it might be better to return to the field for landing. The prospect of returning to make a landing on a snow-covered runway during a snowstorm was not that appealing. John decided to make one more attempt to get on top of the incoming weather. The options were getting fewer and fewer and thoughts were creeping in that perhaps this flight should never have begun.

The airplane climbed to 15,000 feet and was still not over the oncoming cloudbank. Altitude was still being gained at the rate of about 300 feet per minute, which was slow, but it looked as if the airplane would have to climb considerably higher yet to get over this weather front.

Discussions with John's brother on the ground indicated the storm had begun to reach there and light snow had already started to hit the airport. It was doubtful that the ferocity of the storm could be beaten back to the airport before it hit with full force. The last remaining avenue of escape was closing rapidly.

Fortunately, the airplane continued to climb. In this super cooled air, the phenomenal altitude of 16,500 feet was reached! This had to be a record, particularly for a non-supercharged engine that supposedly did not have the ability to go this high. The outside air temperature had dropped to minus 70 degrees below zero! Another ugly factor had just been added.

The heater and defroster were turned all the way up. Even so, it began to get chilly in the cockpit. The heating system was not strong enough to keep the cabin at a comfortable temperature in this extreme cold. Something more was going to have to be done for John to keep warm in this excruciatingly cold outside air temperature.

The autopilot was turned on so the airplane would fly straight and level while John attempted to reach into the back seat to find something additional to put on. A stocking cap and a second down parka were within a stretched out reach. Fortunately these were always carried in the airplane in case of emergency. The parka was placed over John's legs and lap and the stocking cap was a welcome addition for the top of the head and the ears. It had already begun to get bitter cold inside the cabin. At least it was moderately comfortable with the added clothing.

The extreme outside temperature became a major concern to continue the flight. The constant speed prop operates on the oil from the engine sump. This will not circulate into the prop mechanism until the pitch control lever is moved. The oil in the mechanism is located in the forward most part of the nose cone where the cold air going past will cool it quickly. The oil could become congealed to the point the prop would not function properly.

John cycled the prop from low pitch, used for cruising, to high pitch, used for power. This speeded the prop up and down gradually until the hot oil entering the mechanism became effective. Once this occurred, the prop began to function properly. John would have to do this every few minutes in this extreme cold.

The air flowing into the fuel injector from the outside was changed to air flowing from the interior of the engine compartment. This would permit the air being used by the engine to be partially warmed, and keep ice from building in the air intake. Should ice clog the air intake, the engine could stop running, which was certainly not a good idea when the airplane was cruising over mountainous terrain.

Flying at 16,500 feet was just over the progressing weather front. Another call was made to advise John's brother that the flight would continue onward to Kalispell. Shortly after this call, the ground radio went out of range and contact could no longer be made.

The directional bearing to Kalispell was nearly straight into a westerly head wind. The wind became very, very strong. It wasn't realized just how powerful the wind really was until John read the ground speed on the GPS (Global Positioning System). This indicated a startling ground speed of only 44 knots! My God! This meant the head wind was 91 knots! Let's see, 91 knots times 1.151 was about 105 MPH! It was blowing right on the nose of the airplane and forward progress was being severely impeded. At this ground speed, it would take forever to get anywhere, and the amount of fuel being burned per mile would be tremendous.

John made an attempt to improve the affect of this extremely strong headwind by turning 15 degrees to the left from his heading for 10 minutes and then 15 degrees to the right for 10 minutes. When turned 15 degrees off the center of the wind, so the airplane was not flying directly into the wind, the air speed increased by more than 30 knots.

At this still slow pace, it would take more than twice as long to reach Kalispell. A huge amount of fuel was being used each mile of progress. The safe plan was to land at Kalispell and refuel before going on.

The strong wind began to weigh heavily on John's mind. At the speed the airplane was preceding over the ground, the fuel consumption per mile of ground speed was approximately three times normal. If this continued, the airplane would run out of fuel less than half way to Seattle.

Fuel management was going to be even more important than usual on the remainder of this flight. The two fuel gages on the dashboard are notoriously unreliable. The normal plan is to use the two fuel tanks in a pattern, so that it becomes apparent when fuel is getting critically low.

Fuel is used in the left tank for one hour, and then the fuel control knob is switched to the right tank for one and one half hours, then back to the left tank for one and one half hours. At this time the left tank will run dry and the right tank should still have at least 50 minutes of fuel remaining.

The fuel gages are not totally ignored however they are notoriously inaccurate so are not relied on. They are only used to verify the calculated remaining flight time available.

Fuel is a very important item in an airplane. An unknown very wise man once said, "The only time you have too much fuel is when you are on fire".

Using the GPS is a real aid toward fuel management. Included in that little box on the dashboard is a display of the amount of time the engine has been running. It also has an hour and minute count down. When set for a specific time, the count down function will click off the time and will flash a light and ring a buzzer when the time has expired.

The time of one hour was set into the GPS count down function for the left tank. Due to the strong head winds and the poor economy being realized by the engine, fuel usage and the miles left to go would become very important factors. Running out of fuel and having to make a forced landing in this mountainous terrain, by going down through a blind overcast, into the snow and cold, could be downright frightening and is not a good option. Particular precaution was going to be taken to make sure this did not happen due to this horrific wind.

The mountain peaks of Glacier Park were far below, so running into one of them was not a major concern, at least for the moment. Flight continued just above the overcast. The ground could not be seen, and the instruments had to be relied on completely to determine direction of flight and distance to the nearest airport. The GPS was being very valuable for this purpose.

The flight continued at this slow pace for seemingly hours. The airplane was turned 15 degrees to the left of center and flown for 10 minutes and then turned to the right 15 degrees for another 10 minutes. The sky above was bright blue, but the overcast underneath was solid white. It was as if the entire world had turned upside down.

The buzzer for the count down timer went off indicating the airplane had been airborne for one hour. Fuel was switched from the left to the right tank and the GPS was reset for a one and one half-hour countdown.

Kalispell should have been reached by this time. The GPS indicated the half way mark had only just been achieved. Fuel was being used as never before and little progress forward was being made.

It seemed to be a long time until the GPS and DME (distance measuring equipment) indicated Kalispell was just a few miles further on. Familiar landmarks could not be seen since nearly all below was solid white. The north end of Flathead Lake was the only clear area, but everything else was completely overcast. The airplane was pointed toward the clearing and a let down to pattern altitude was begun in preparation for landing at Glacier Park International. An attempt was going to be made to fly under the cloudbank to find the airport and make a landing.

The ceiling was high enough to get under the overcast; however, as the airplane descended it began to get foggier and foggier. The closer John flew to the airport the thicker it became. Visibility was deteriorating rapidly, but it appeared adequate to make a landing.

Closer to the airport the ceiling appeared to be lowering. If a landing was made, it just might not be possible to take off again. Being stranded here was not appealing, so John made a decision to continue on. This decision was one more poor decision that John should never have even considered.

The wind had died down a little and was now blowing at about 40 or 50 knots aloft. John calculated that a flight to Sand Point, Idaho could be made with an adequate fuel reserve remaining, provided the wind was not too strong.

The Flathead Valley was clear, but the surrounding mountains were shrouded in fog and overcast. Rather than climb back to 16,500 feet to get over the top of the overcast, the route of flight was changed to fly over Flathead Lake and up the Thompson River Valley. This is a little longer, but it is much lower and wouldn't demand the time and fuel to climb back to the top.

The temperature had warmed considerably. It was now only 10 below rather than minus 70 as it had been.

As the flight continued to the south end of Flathead Lake, the strong wind was coming from the side of the airplane, rather than the front and was not impeding progress as it had been previously. Unfortunately this changed back to a direct head wind as a turn was made to fly up the Thompson Valley. With this strong wind, the flight to Sand Point should take about an hour.

Fuel was already being burned a second time from the left tank, which was almost empty. If the strong wind continued, fuel would be exhausted just beyond Sand Point. Much more fuel was being used than originally predicted. A great tightness in the pit of John's stomach was beginning to be felt.

The GPS was reprogrammed to guide up the Thompson Valley in order to fly as directly to Sand Point as possible. Hopefully this would conserve fuel. Fog remained low over the Valley; however, it remained high enough to be able to fly in the valley and still fly legally. Visibility forward was restricted to about five miles. The airplane was being flown down one side of the valley in case the weather deteriorated and it became necessary to turn around. This would allow room for this maneuver, if the need should arise. The wind down the side of the valley was always less than down the center as well. This would help conserve fuel, which was quickly becoming a major concern. That tight feeling in the pit of John's stomach was beginning to turn into a hard knot.

Power was cut back to 2100 RPM and the manifold pressure was reduced to 21 inches. The mixture control was adjusted back slowly until the cylinder head temperature reached its maximum. This would provide 65 % power and would also conserve fuel, without cutting the speed too drastically.

Minutes seemed to grow into hours. The wind was not diminishing as John had hoped. The engine was burning much more fuel per mile than normal, and the wind was still keeping the ground speed very low.

The prop continued to be cycled every few minutes to allow hot oil to circulate into the prop mechanism. The outside air temperature was still fluctuating between -10 and - 20 below zero. The heater and defroster were keeping the chill off, but it was still cold inside the airplane.

Suddenly the engine began to sputter and quit completely. The silence was deafening! All that could be heard was the pounding of John's heart. The nose of the airplane was dropped in order to maintain the glide speed of 110 MPH. The left wing tank had run out of fuel. Approximately 50 minutes flying time remained in the right tank – or maybe less because of the headwind.

The electric fuel pump was turned on as the fuel selector was frantically switched from the left to the right tank. The engine came back to life with the sweetest sound ever heard, drowning out the strong thumping in John's chest. The airplane was flying once again, but the fuel used was much more than he had calculated. There was only a maximum of 10 gallons of fuel remaining of which at least 2 gallons were unusable.

Sweat was beginning to run down John's forehead. Fuel usage calculations began to pierce his mind. There appeared to be enough fuel to reach Sand Point, but there would only be a very small reserve.

The airplane had been in the air for more than four hours now and was burning the last of the reserve fuel. Theoretically the fuel remaining in the right tank would last just under an hour. Sand Point was still 45 minutes away. Tension was mounting with perhaps less than 50 minutes of fuel in the right tank and nothing in the left.

Sand Point was called on the radio. There was no answer. After a few minutes the radio was tried again. Still there was no answer. Mountains were on both sides of the airplane, and it was possible they were blocking transmission.

An agonizing half hour later, Lake Pend Oreille appeared at the head end of the canyon and the City of Sand Point could be seen as the airplane flew out onto the lake. The radio was tried one more time. Sand Point Unicom answered. It was not the answer John had hoped for!

It had snowed more than 12 inches during the last few hours and the runway was completely covered. The airport maintenance crew had broken down their snowplow, and a landing was completely out of the question!

Bad luck was still holding. Fear was beginning to grip John in earnest. The airplane was already fuel critical and there was no place to land!

What was the nearest airport? Could the fuel hold out until reaching another airport? Felts Field in Spokane was too far and the airplane would definitely run out of fuel before reaching there.

With very nervous fingers, the emergency button was pushed on the GPS and a list of airports was scrolled through to find the closest one. Coeur d'Alene was closest and was 30 miles away. At the current speed, the GPS indicated it would take another 5 minutes to get there. My God! Could he make it there without running out of fuel?

The airplane had been flying on the last 30 minutes of reserve fuel for nearly 25 minutes now. This was going to be close! There was no assurance the engine would keep running with the fuel so low. Sweat was beginning to run and that knot in the pit of John's stomach just became much bigger.

Power was cut even more as Coeur d'Alene Unicom was called on the radio. Coeur d'Alene advised the airport was being plowed and was still closed to traffic. John advised he was "fuel critical" and needed to land immediately. Coeur d'Alene Unicom said, "We have one runway plowed and we can open this for you. You will have to wait until we plow out the fueling area before we can fuel your airplane". John said, "That sounds good to me. Just get me on the ground!"

Boy was the sweat rolling! How could he be sweating when it was so cold in the airplane? The GPS was clicking off the miles and tenths of miles left to go to touchdown. Every mile seemed to be an agony. Where was that airport? The engine must have been running on the very last fumes in the tank by now. Nervousness had turned to fear and fear to near panic.

Where could an emergency landing be made? This would be difficult with all the snow. The airplane could easily end up upside down and rolled into a ball. If an emergency landing were to be made, perhaps it would be better to leave the wheels up and land in the snow. This seemed to be safer than the alternative.

The airport was getting closer. "Oh baby! Don't let me down now!" John could see the runway in the distance. "Was the distance too far?" A call was made on the radio announcing to any other aircraft in the area that a straight in landing to the west was about to be made in a fuel critical airplane. John's hands were shaking so badly the control column could hardly be held.

Airspeed was reduced to 100 MPH and the descent to the airstrip was begun even though the airport could not yet be seen. The flaps were lowered to 5 degrees. The wheels were purposely left up for fear too much drag would be created, using too much fuel. Running out just short of touch down would be disastrous.

As the airport came into full view, a little silent prayer was made that there was enough fuel left in the tanks to make it to the threshold. The seconds seemed like hours. The next few moments reaching the airport seemed like an eternity. If the engine could only keep running for just a few more minutes….

The threshold finally arrived and the wheels were lowered just before touchdown. The airplane settled to the pavement with a slight thud, AND THE ENGINE WAS STILL RUNNING!

What a relief! The last drop of fuel must have been used coming in. The engine was shut down and the airplane sat next to the fueling area while the deep snow was being plowed. Then the airplane was pulled to the fuel pump by hand.

The remaining fuel in the tanks was almost un-measurable! The remainder of the trip home would have to wait until another day. John had had enough for one day.

STRONG WINDS AND SEVERE DOWN DRAFTS

The brand-new Piper Cherokee Arrow lifted off easily from the runway at Crest Airpark near Seattle and began to climb into a beautiful blue sky. John was heading over the mountains of Western Washington, across the plains of Eastern Washington, across the panhandle of Idaho, over the extremely rugged Rocky Mountains of Western Montana and out onto the great planes of Eastern Montana. This distance was to take about three hours. Final destination was the small town of Conrad, Montana.

John pulled back on the control column and stood the airplane on it's propeller in order to climb as fast as possible and reach the intended cruising altitude of 7,500 feet. This altitude or greater was necessary in order to cross the highest mountain peaks of Stampede Pass located in the heart of the Cascade Mountains. This mountain ridge, and the pass through it, separated the mountainous area of western Washington from the flat irrigated farm land of eastern Washington.

Dark clouds were seen in the distance and they had boulders in them at any lower altitude. Lower flights would have been extremely dangerous.

This route had been flown many times, but this time the flight was destined to be more exciting than usual.

Actually, the airplane being flown was not new. It was only new to John. It was a 1976 model that had been purchased six months previously. The engine was near its TBO (time between overhauls) at the time of purchase and was immediately replaced with a 200-horse power remanufactured engine. All moving parts were new and it had been well broken in and was running like a top.

An instrument panel mounted GPS (Global Positioning System) satellite navigation system had been added which was coupled, or directly connected, to the autopilot. This fantastic and innovative equipment would allow the airplane to be flown to as many as 15 waypoints, hands off the controls. John had just begun to learn how to use all of this new and exciting equipment. Navigating the airplane from point to point was made so much easier.

The weather the previous week had been unusually cold. Light snow had fallen over the low-lying hills of the Cascade Range and it had begun to freeze nearly every night.

The outside air temperature this morning in the Seattle area had been relatively warm and was hovering in the high 40's. As the airplane began to ascend into the sky the temperature began to fall with every foot of altitude gained.

At 5,000 feet the temperature had dropped to below freezing and was heading much lower as the climb continued. At 7,500 feet the airplane was over all the mountain peaks in the immediate area and the outside air temperature had dropped to ten degrees below zero. Even at this elevation the temperature was exceptionally low for early winter.

The extreme temperature was bothersome but had not been the only enemy rearing it's ugly head. The ferocity of the wind had become a much bigger threat. It had begun to blow from the west at around 60 knots.

This was not too bothersome initially because it was a tail wind. It was a little strong but had made the airplane move much faster over the ground. It was to become an increasing concern as this trip progressed.

Fortunately John's direction of flight had been eastward and nearly the same direction as the wind was going. It had began to give the airplane a grand push and this was about to generate a series of bazaar events.

Clouds had been building as the flight continued toward Eastern Washington. The flight plan had been filed for a landing at Coeur d'Alene, Idaho where John's friends were to be visited before proceeding across Idaho into Montana.

Three additional mountain crests were to be crossed between Coeur d' Alene, Idaho, Kalispell, Montana and onward to Conrad, Montana. These were the Continental Divide on the border of Idaho and Montana, a ridge of the Rocky Mountains just prior to Kalispell, Montana and the Great Rocky Mountains of Glacier National Park, just prior to flying out onto the farm lands of eastern Montana.

It was necessary to climb to 11,500 feet to cross these three mountain ridges. This was high for most light aircraft, but was nothing at all for the "new" Cherokee Arrow. Previous flights in this aircraft had been quite comfortable over this same route and John was a competent pilot with hundreds of hours of mountain flying.

Prior to reaching Coeur d'Alene, which was to be the destination for the evening, the clouds had thickened and a solid overcast had moved in behind John. The airplane had to be raised to 13,500 feet to break into the clear above the broken clouds ahead.

When reaching 11,500 feet it had become necessary to use supplemental oxygen. The green bottle mounted in the back seat was turned on and breathing was through the attaching hose and small mask.

When Coeur d'Alene had come into view the broken clouds below had become thinner and the view of the ground had improved. A dark, threatening cloud bank could be seen in the distance, perhaps 20 miles to the west. Flight Watch had advised further flying that day had not been advisable and John had been happy to land at Coeur d'Alene and wait for better weather.

Shortly after John's arrival on the ground for the evening, the weather deteriorated considerably. Landing and waiting for better weather had been the smart thing to have done. Problems for the next leg of the trip were about to materialize, however.

By early next morning low clouds had covered the entire sky and ground fog completely permeated the Coeur d'Alene basin for the next few days. Mountains to the east were no longer visible. VFR flight was completely out of the question for the next three days.

On the fourth day the weather improved. The surface wind had increased and this had blown a few holes in the clouds. The holes were just large enough for the airplane to climb through to get into the clear air above the large broken cloud banks.

The Rocky Mountains just west of Coeur de Alene were the next to be crossed. John had great expectations of reaching his final destination in about two hours of flight. There had been little indication this was the beginning of a real terror adventure.

As the flight had progressed the large cumulous clouds began to rise. It had become necessary to climb even higher to get over their tops. The old "get there 'itas" was a strong incentive to continue on. The half way point between Coeur de Alene had been passed and it had become a shorter distance to continue to Conrad than it would have been to return to Coeur de Alene. The strong wind pushing the airplane was a strong incentive for Ray to continue since it would have been hard to fight against this wind while going the other way.

When the Cherokee had reached 14,500 feet, John was still not over the top of the broken clouds. Since this was the theoretical ceiling of the Cherokee Arrow, John did not known just how much higher the airplane was capable of climbing. It had become an interesting challenge for him to find out just how high this airplane could actually fly.

Since the airplane was still climbing at a rate of 300 feet per minute, the flight had continued in an attempt to get over the top of the huge clouds. Flying would be much better than going around each one. Without supplemental oxygen, this flight would have been impossible.

The ceiling defined in the pilot's handbook for the Cherokee Arrow is 14,500 feet. The airplane had exceeded this altitude and was still climbing. If it had not been possible to reach the tops soon, it would have been necessary to turn around and go back to Coeur d'Alene as the clouds were getting thicker. Even this would have been difficult because the weather appeared to be socking in behind the airplane.

An increasingly powerful wind had risen. If a return trip was to have been made, this would have to be fought all the way back to Coeur d'Alene. If John had turned around, this strong wind would have been right on the nose of the airplane. This would have greatly impeded forward progress and would have caused an extraordinary amount of fuel to be burned.

The clouds in the direction of John's flight had become thicker and the ground could not be seen quite so often. The nose of the airplane was pointed toward the sky and the slow climb continued to see if an even higher altitude could be reached so the clouds would not have to be gone around. 15,500 feet had come and gone and the airplane was still climbing. The airplane was now 1,000 feet above its published ceiling.

The wind seemed to increase with every foot of elevation gained. It was now blowing at the phenomenal strength of 74 knots. Fortunately, it was still going the same direction as John's route of flight. Ground speed had picked up from the normal 160 MPH to 234 MPH! This was faster than this airplane had ever been flown, and the excitement of it all made John's heart pound a little. The wind was yet to become even stronger.

Ironically the airplane was still slowly gaining altitude even though it was far above its normal ceiling. The outside air temperature had reached 22 degrees below zero. The wind must have been blowing up over the western side of the mountains and was shoving the airplane to a higher altitude with its huge rising air current. The extreme cold air, the strong wind and the new engine installed in the airplane were allowing the airplane to far exceed its normal flight characteristics.

The cloud tops were getting higher and higher. At the same time the rate of climb was getting slower and slower. Reaching the cloud tops was becoming more difficult. The airplane was performing exceptionally well as it continued it slow climb into the sky.

The incredible altitude of 17,500 feet was reached! No one was ever going to believe this. This was 3,000 feet above the published ceiling for this aircraft. Another 500 feet and the airplane would be in Positive Air Space where it would be necessary to revise the VFR (Visual Flight Rules) flight plan and file IFR (Instrument Flight Rules).

John made a decision to stay at this altitude and continue on, rather than to turn around and have to fight this horrendous wind going in the opposite direction. The airplane was almost over the top of the clouds and it might be possible to stay at this altitude to make it the rest of the way across the mountains to the great plains of eastern Montana without flying into them.

John made a call to Flight Watch on the radio and requested current weather conditions in central Montana. They immediately responded indicating the great plains were clear; however there were very strong winds at higher elevations. Only the relatively short remainder of the flight over the mountains had to be negotiated above the broken clouds.

John glance at the ground speed being displayed on the GPS and received a real shock. This indicated the airplane was moving over the ground at a phenomenal rate of 267 MPH! The extremely strong tail wind had increased to more than 100 MPH! The airplane was traveling over the ground at more than 100 miles per hour faster than it normally would cruise. It was giving the airplane a tremendous push and the engine wasn't burning much fuel in the process.

Slowly the tops of the clouds began to lower. As they lowered, descent was possible to 11,500 feet. This was still a thousand feet above the highest peaks of the Glacier Park area mountains. Even though all peaks could not always be seen, the visibility was good enough for safe flying and the airplane was at least 1,000 feet above the highest ones.

Letdown was planned as soon as the airplane flew out of the mountains onto the plains. It should have only been another quarter-hour or so before reaching this point. The descent to landing pattern altitude from the extreme altitude of the airplane would take a considerable amount of time. The wind was blowing fiercely in excess of 100 MPH, right directly on the tail of the airplane.

Flying so high and so fast would never have been believed by any of John's friends and family. He would have to decide whether to even tell them about this because he seriously doubted they would believe him anyway.

As the airplane rushed across the ground, high above the Rockies, thoughts entered John's mind about how in the world this point in his flying career had ever been reached. How many years had it been since he first climbed into that all wood and fabric tail dragger to take his first flying lesson? His first solo had been in 1947. My God, that had been more than 50 years ago!

Along with his initial flight instruction so many years ago, John had been taught aerobatics. His first instructor had been a Major in the US Marine Corps during World War II and had flown from aircraft carriers. Aerobatics were a big part of his early teaching and spot landings on the threshold of the runway were his specialty. Since that time, John's many years of flying had developed his flying proficiency and had honed his flying skills well.

All different types of aerobatic maneuvers were taught in the early days of John's flying carrier. It certainly had not been like today's instruction. Nearly all-general aviation airplanes today are restricted from practically all such maneuvers. Most small airplanes are not certified to perform such aerobatics. The Piper Cherokee Arrow was no exception. In this aircraft, as in most other general aviation aircraft, all Aerobatics which require a bank in excess of 60 degree are restricted. This restriction eliminates spins, which a lot of older pilots feel should be included in the curriculum for all new pilots.

During early flight training years ago, spins had been required in order to qualify for the Private Pilot Certificate. In addition to being taught this maneuver, loops, chandelles, Cuban eights, snap rolls, slow rolls and all types of recoveries from unusual attitudes had been stressed. Even inverted flight was attempted, but the small airplanes of those days were not powerful enough and would fall shortly after being inverted and go into a dive and a recovery had to be made. The engines were not powerful enough to maintain inverted flight.

Knowing where the airplane was at all times, particularly in unusual attitudes, was strongly stressed by the instructors. Better pilots were thought to have natural instincts for knowing where the airplane was at all times in relation to straight and level flight. Performance of these maneuvers had all but been forgotten by John, but this was about to play a heavy part in the events of the next few minutes.

Suddenly, without warning, the airplane emerged into a dense fog. Inadvertently an invisible unseen cloud had been flown into. All of a sudden the only visual reference John had was the inside of the windshield. The view through the window was solid white. It was as if a white curtain had suddenly been pulled down over the entire airplane. Visibility forward was no farther than the inside of the cockpit!

Having no visual reference of the horizon made it impossible to tell up from down and tension mounted immediately. John's heart began to pound like a base drum as he quickly glued his gaze to the instruments on the panel in front of him.

When confronted with this type of situation, the natural tendency is to over control the airplane. In most cases this is absolutely the wrong thing to do. This will usually cause the inexperienced pilot to input wrong directions into the controls.

John's surprise was nearly total as he inadvertently flew into the cloud. Momentary confusion caused control of the airplane to be by instinct only and absolutely the wrong input was made to the controls.

Not being able to see the horizon, the control column was unconsciously pulled back, which made the airplane climb. The control wheel must have also been turned slightly to the right, as the airplane banked crosswise to the extremely strong wind. The airplane flipped sideways in the sudden turbulence and became caught in a severe down draft.

The air must have been boiling down the far side of the mountain range causing the airplane to plummet nearly straight down as it was caught in the grip of an extremely violent wind.

Nearly complete spatial disorientation was experienced during several seconds of this blind flying. The attitude of the airplane could not be determined without looking at the instruments. There was absolutely no visual reference to the outside world.

Pulling back on the control column and turning slightly to the right seemed the correct thing to do. John's senses were completely confused by the inability to see and the suddenness of being thrown into this unusual attitude.

The engine began to race. It became apparent the airplane was in a severe nosedive toward the ground. This was big trouble and the shear terror of it hit John like a sever blow to the stomach. The wrong thing had been done which had made the situation worse! It was a struggle to gain control of his senses and to begin to do the right thing.

Instinctively the throttle was pulled back and the controls were released from his hand. Normally this would have allowed the airplane to stabilize itself. Someone once said, "The airplane knows more about flying than we will ever know". Most of the time turning loose the controls will return the airplane to upright, wing level flight. Then it is usually possible to gently push forward on the control column to put the airplane in a shallow dive to pick up any lost speed. Then a gentle pull back on the control column will usually return the aircraft to normal level flight.

The control column was turned loose by John but this time it didn't work. The strong down draft threw everything around the cockpit including the pilot like a rag doll. The seatbelt and shoulder strap began to pull hard on John's chest and it became apparent the airplane had become inverted. There was at least a two inches gap between the seat of John's paints and the seat cushion. The engine began to rev and dirt from the floor began to fly around the inside of the cockpit. The microphone came down off the hook and hit John in the head.

Nothing could be seen out the front of the windshield and the attitude of the airplane could not be determined by visual reference. The instruments were the only means of determining what the airplane was doing. John glued his eyes to the dash board.

The extremely powerful down draft had taken hold of the airplane and wasn't about to turn loose. The airplane was being carried along with it in the inverted position with the nose high. This was a terrible attitude for the airplane to be in because aerodynamically it was no longer flying and gaining control would be extremely difficult.

Gripped tightly by the down draft, the airplane was dropping out of the sky like a lead sled. Extreme fear had nearly taken over and John's eyes had become as big as saucers.

It was a struggle using all his senses and strong will to gain his composure. Thoughts of John's early aerobatic training so many years ago fleeted through his mind. Gaining control of the airplane was much harder due to the surprise of it all, the lack of visual reference outside the airplane, and the sudden plummeting of the airplane inverted toward disaster.

All life seemed to depend on making the right moves to affect recovery. Something had to be done to roll the airplane upright and then to somehow fly out of this down draft and fog—and it had to be done now!

Where were those mountains? Was this down draft going to drive the airplane straight down onto the rocks? Still nothing could be seen. No more time was left to think. Action had to be taken now to gain immediate control.

The control column was frantically pulled back. This had the opposite effect it would have had during normal flight. It lowered the nose of the airplane into a shallow, inverted dive. Fortunately this was the right thing to do. A little self-composure was gained by the reaction of the airplane. As the nose went down, the right rudder pedal was stepped on with all John's might. The airplane began to slowly roll to the right as it fought against the powerful wind. It was still in a slight downward dive. As the airplane righted itself, the left rudder pedal was pushed to stop the roll. The airplane stabilized laterally, but continued in a nose down severe descent. Aerodynamically it was now flying, but was still held firmly inside the powerful down draft.

Partial control of the airplane had been gained, but it was still heading down with absolutely no visibility to tell where the mountains were.

During John's previous mountain flying training, it had been stressed that while caught in a severe down draft, no attempt to pull out of it should be made. Unless the airplane has an extremely powerful engine, pulling out of it will be nearly impossible. This would only fight against the wind, and make things worse. The airplane could easily loose stability and little or no control could be exerted over it. The best solution was said to be to fly the airplane down with the wind until the down draft reaches the bottom of the mountain and begins to curve up the valley. This was all echoing in John's mind, but it was hard for him to overcome sever panic and make himself do the right thing when it was unknown whether the airplane was even in a valley.

If there was a bottom to this it could not be felt. Doing the correct thing to survive is much harder when nothing can be seen and the instruments are the only means to recovery.

The tendency to pull out of the dive had to be fought against as the airplane was pointed down. The power setting was adjusted to low cruise, and attention was immediately glued to the instrument panel. Rate of decent was 3,000 feet per minute or perhaps even more. It was impossible to tell accurately since the indicator needle on the rate of climb instrument was pegged as far as it would go. Fear of crashing into the mountains was almost overwhelming and John's entire body was as tense as a steel post.

Slowly, and certainly not fast enough for comfort, the descent rate began to decrease. The nose of the airplane was raised slightly and the airplane slowly began to fly forward as well as down. Gradually it became possible to keep the airplane straight and level as it began to fly out of the down draft. Still nothing could be seen. The wind was still pushing the airplane at a ground speed rate in excess of 200 MPH, but the wings were finally level and the airplane hadn't run into a mountain—yet!

The prop pitch was set to full fine and the throttle was pushed to the firewall. This would provide maximum power available. The nose was raised as much as was dared in an attempt to establish a climb. John's hands on the controls were shaking like an exotic dancer. The airplane had been taken down a long way and the tops of the mountains had to be very close. Climbing as fast as the airplane would possibly climb seemed the safest way to keep from going into those hidden rock cliffs.

This drama was not over yet. A major problem still existed because nothing could be seen out the windshield and it was impossible to tell where the rocks were in relation to the altitude. The airplane could easily be in a valley and heading straight for the rocky peaks.

No attempted to turn around was going to be made as the airplane was still too high to be out of the clouds and it was undoubtedly below the surrounding mountain peaks. The extremely strong 100-MPH wind would have to be fought against if turning around. This could also cause the airplane to fly right back into the down draft. Even making a turn sideways to the wind without proper visibility could result in a second loss of control of the airplane. The adrenaline rush was making John's hands shake and the fear of flying towards disaster completely blind was absolutely overwhelming.

A lot of altitude had been lost during the sudden dive toward the ground. Hopefully the airplane was still high enough to be over the top of the mountains.

A glance at the altimeter indicated the airplane was well below 8,000 feet. The peaks in this range of mountains were over 9,000 feet tall. The down draft had taken the airplane down more than 4,000 feet, and it was impossible to tell what the surrounding terrain was like.

Eventually clear air would be reached as the airplane emerged into the flat country on the eastern side of the mountains. How far was this going to be? Could the airplane climb high enough, soon enough, to be over the top of the terrain?

Flying completely blind like this was extremely nerve wracking, particularly after the shock of the down draft and overcoming the loss of control of the airplane. A lot had happened during the past few minutes. A great deal of progress had been made to recover, but John's emotions had better not get the best of him now.

Prior to this incident, John had been flying VFR (Visual Flight Rules) and should file IFR (Instrument Flight Rules) so that Flight Center could follow him on radar. They would be able to assist by keeping him from running into another airplane or mountain, but first he had to have kept the airplane under control by flying solely by the instruments. Even though it was illegal to be flying in the clouds, the rule is FLY THE AIRPLANE FIRST – then worry about the paperwork. It doesn't do much good to notify flight control, who can't understand the situation you are in, and couldn't do anything about it if they did.

John's thoughts had been focused on what might be out in front. Where were the mountains? Was he high enough? Was there another mountain peak in front of him? Was he about to run into it?

John's mind was racing with fearful thoughts. He had to make himself assume the airplane was still over the tops of the mountains and not headed for solid rock. If the alternative was true it would all be over soon anyway. His hands were really shaking, but the airplane had to be flown out of this predicament.

Flying blind for these few minutes seemed like several hours. John's hands were shaking so badly it was difficult for him to hold onto the control column and his nerves were about to jump out of his skin.

Suddenly the sun pierced through the fog and the shape of the clouds could be seen. This was somewhat of a relief, but it was an even greater relief when a few minutes later the sky began to clear and the airplane emerged completely from the clouds.

About 1,000 feet directly below was US Highway 2. The inverted plummet had been over the eastern edge of the mountains as suspected. The great drop had occurred down the near side of a large valley and the airplane was about to fly out onto the plains of western Montana. Wow! The grand ordeal was finally over except for the shaking! It had been an extremely lucky adventure.

With all the hundreds of hours spent in the left-hand seat as "Pilot in Command" of a complex class airplane, this had been John's most embarrassing moment. The airplane had got completely away from him. The suddenness of it had caught him completely by surprise. Initially the wrong things had been done. This had shaken him to the core but there was also a great deal of gratification in knowing that his former training had pulled him through and had provided knowledge enough for him to have eventually done the right thing.

There was still 50 miles left to go to John's final destination. The Cherokee's Ground speed was still above 200 MPH. The remainder of the flight required only another 15 minutes.

The wind had begun to decrease as descent for letdown began. By the time the traffic pattern had been entered for landing the wind had died down to a more respectable 30 MPH, with wind gusts to 40. This was still extreme and a crosswind landing was completely out of the question. Fortunately the wind was blowing nearly straight down the center of the runway.

The landing gear was lowered, but the flaps were kept in the retracted position in order to land in this high, gusty wind. An extra long final approach was made and the approach speed was held 20 miles per hour faster than normal. The landing was perhaps not one of John's usual whisper landings but against this strong wind, at least the airplane reached the ground in one piece.

Wow! What a relief! John was safely on the ground and the airplane had come to a stop. John's legs had turned to jelly by this time and it was impossible for him to get out of the airplane for the next few moments. When finally John's legs would support his weight, he moved the airplane into a hanger where it sat for the next three weeks of bad weather.

DON'T TRY BARGAINING WITH THE ICE MACHINE

The weather ahead appeared to be improving. The walk around Coeur d'Alene, Idaho Airport, and the candy bars hurriedly eaten in the FBO office, had been somewhat reviving from the riggers of the first leg of John's journey. Remaining was another two-hour leg to be flown to reach home base. John made the decision to forge onward even though he was extremely tired.

The flight from eastern Montana had been rigorous and tiring, having to fight the exceptionally powerful headwinds. It had taken five hours to fly to Coeur d'Alene, which would have ordinarily taken three hours. Had it been known what was in store for the next leg of the trip, the airplane would have never left the ground the rest of that day. Unfortunately the worst of this flight was yet to come.

That old "get home-itas" can generate serious problems for the unwary. Strong headwinds aloft were forecast for the route ahead. This would impede progress, but did not appear to be a real serious threat. Unknown at this time, the phenomenon referred to as "The Pacific Ice Machine" in the Pacific Northwest was. John was about to encounter this!

This phenomenon is quite often present on the West Side of the Cascade Mountains during the winter months, and is referred to as the "ice machine". This weather abnormality can cause a nasty encounter for any pilot inadvertently caught in it.

The "ice machine" condition is created by warm, moist air from the Pacific Ocean pushing up and over the Cascade Mountains by the prevailing westerly winds. The mountains rapidly cool the warm air and the moisture within is condensed into freezing fog. It appears as a fog bank and must be stayed away from by all. A pilot inadvertently flying into this will immediately loose all visual reference and will pick up ice on the airplane instantly.

An airplane stumbling into this condition can be in serious trouble. Ice can build extremely fast on the leading edge surfaces of the wings and the fuselage. Excessive weight suddenly added, along with deformed wing surfaces, can rapidly destroy the lifting capacity of the wings

In order to fly, air has to flow smoothly over the top and bottom of an airfoil. The presence of ice, along with the added weight, can easily disturb this airflow and can rapidly place the airplane in close proximity to a stall. Too much ice on the wings without anti-icing capability could place the airplane in serious harms way.

Leaving Coeur d'Alene on the last leg of John's flight, the mountains gave way to the plains of eastern Washington. The sky cleared somewhat, and the headwind died down a few knots from what it had been. Progress was still slow. Flying west into the prevailing winds, the headwind was directly on the nose of the airplane at 60 knots. Except for slowing the ground speed of the airplane down a great deal, this was not the real enemy. Freezing fog was about to be encountered.

The rate of ice accumulation on an airplane is important. If it builds slowly, there is some time to deal with it. If it is "wham", and there is one inch built immediately, something has to be done about it NOW! If the airplane is in the freezing level, it must be flown out of it at once. The ice can't be moved, so the airplane must be moved out of the ice. A 180-degree turn in this instance is not a disgrace. It may be a lifesaver.

One other condition exists, which can cause instant concern, especially for relatively inexperienced pilots and those who seldom fly instruments. When an airplane enters cloud or fog, the pilot may experience "spatial disorientation". To keep this from happening, the pilot must immediately glue his attention to the instrument panel in order to keep the airplane flying straight and level.

Several instruments are required for this purpose, but perhaps the most beneficial is the artificial horizon. When the actual horizon can not be seen, there is no reference for the pilot's mind to base straight and level flight. The artificial horizon must be used to enable the pilot to have visual presentation of the actual horizon. If spatial disorientation does occur, within 30 seconds or less, the airplane will almost always go into what is scarily referred to as a "death spiral". Significant altitude can be lost, or the airplane can stall, go into a spin, causing the necessity for a fast recovery.

A small number of pilots over the years have found themselves caught in the "ice machine", which can contain both of the above problems at the same time, icing and spatial disorientation. Some pilots have had major problems escaping from the clutches of these.

John had one more mountain range to be crossed on the last leg of this trip. This was the Cascade Mountains of western Washington which was near his home base. The temperature had been below freezing at higher elevations, but there had been no reports of icing conditions. Unknown to John, the ice machine was much in existence and was preparing its sinister load.

John called Seattle Flight Watch on the radio to check the weather going into Seattle. Flight Watch indicated winds aloft for six, nine and twelve thousand feet were more intense at higher altitude. He would encounter lighter headwinds the lower he flew.

John was cruising at 8,500 feet where the airplane could safely be flown to cross the Pass in the Cascade Mountains. The nose of the airplane was pointed toward Stampede Pass and the throttle and fuel mixture levers were adjusted to 75 % power.

Once across the Cascade Mountain Range, let down could begin in preparation for landing at Crest Airpark, near the outskirts of Seattle. The route of flight was to be over Stampede Pass, which was directly in line with Crest Airpark. This was home base, and all would be happy for his arrival after this long and difficult flight. Stampede Pass was the lowest and shortest route through this area of the mountains, so the intent was to fly over this Pass and into Crest Airpark.

Stampede Pass could be crossed as low as 8,500 feet going west and 7,500 feet going east. All VFR (Visual Flight Rules) aircraft were required to fly even altitudes plus 500 feet while going west, and odd altitudes plus 500 feet going east. This is required for traffic separation.

The weather had been relatively clear as the flight progressed over the flat country of Eastern Washington, until arriving closer to the Cascade Mountains. A layer of clouds could be seen above the mountains. Perhaps the airplane could squeeze under these and still make it over Stampede Pass. Not having to climb another 4,000 feet to get over the cloudbank would save a lot of time and fuel.

As the cloudbank drew nearer, it became obvious it would not be possible to fly under it and still remain above the mountain peaks. The control column was pulled back and John began a cruise climb.

By 10,000 feet the airplane was over the top of the cloudbank and the flight could be continued over Stampede Pass. Just beyond the crest of the Pass, the clouds began to dissipate, and a let down was begun in clear air. The GPS indicated Crest Airpark was 40 miles away. A slow decent to pattern altitude would take another 20 minutes.

Seattle Flight Watch was called again for an update on the weather at Seattle Tacoma International Airport. Visibility was reported to be five miles, with a low ceiling. Unfortunately Sea-Tac Airport was IFR (Instrument Flight Rules) and a landing could not be made there since this flight was VFR (Visual Flight Rules).

It may be possible to get under the ceiling and still make it into Crest Airpark VFR. It was often quite possible to do this and still be legal. The airport at Crest was higher than Sea-Tac and it was a non-controlled airport. Minimum allowable conditions for landing were less since it was a non-controlled airport. If a landing could not be made at Crest, John planned to return over the mountain pass and land at Ellensburg where the weather was clear.

Once over the Pass, flying down the center of a large valley would make the decent to 4,000 feet possible. Tops of the mountains were above the airplane on both sides.

With little warning, John flew into a dense fog! The fog was so thick nothing could be seen beyond the front of the airplane. Only half of the wings were visible out the side windows, and the front windshield was solid white.

The last view of the mountains had eliminated any possibility of a safe 180-degree turn to go back. Descent of the airplane was halted, and the control column was pulled back putting the airplane in a gentle climb. Immediately attention was glued to the instruments. Going into a "death spiral" and losing altitude, or going into a slight turn could put the airplane right into the mountains.

Nothing at all could be seen out the front window. This was a terrible feeling, and so unexpected. It was impossible to tell where the mountains were. The airplane had to be flown blindly by flying on the instruments until this could be worked out. Where were those mountains? Could the airplane continue to be flown straight-ahead without running into one of them? How far must the airplane be flown until out of the mountains and out of danger? How close to Crest Airpark could the airplane be flown before being clear of the mountains, which would permit a let down to lower altitude? All kinds of unknowns were racing through John's mind.

A cold sweat was breaking out on his forehead and near panic was beginning to grip in earnest. Absolutely nothing could be seen out the windshield except solid white. The only avenue open seemed to be to rely on the GPS for direction since it was set on a direct track to Crest.

My God, the airplane had turned 20 degrees off the track to the right! Could a turn be made back to the track without running into the mountains, or would the mountains be run into if flight were continued 20 degrees off to the right? A frantic decision was made in what must have taken less time to think about than it did to do. It seemed more logical to turn back to the original track and then to follow the GPS toward Crest. Hopefully the airplane was not flying directly into a mountain. It was impossible to tell in this heavy fog. John became extremely tense and was gripped with almost paralyzing fear.

According to the artificial horizon the airplane was still in a gentle climb. How much higher must the airplane climb to clear the top of the mountain peaks? 5,000 feet had been reached, but the airplane was still not above the fog. Moving John's attention from the instruments long enough to look at the aerial map to determine how high the mountains were in this area was completely out of the question. He must fly the airplane blindly on instruments.

Several minutes went by with fear building with every moment. The airplane flew on through the fog, but nothing happened. Still nothing could be seen past the nose of the airplane.

My God! What was that on the windshield? Ice was building from the bottom and sides. Even to look at the wings placed fear in John's mind. He was almost afraid of what he might see. Ice was building up on these too! It must have been at least half an inch thick on the leading edge. The airplane had to be taken down to warmer air immediately. Flight Watch had indicated the freezing level was at 5,000 feet.

In this fog, how close could the airplane get to Crest before John could make a let down and still expect to be clear of the mountains? The GPS indicated Crest was 15.2 nautical miles away. If a mountain was not run into, the airplane still couldn't continue to fly with ice building up on it as it was. John had to get the airplane out of the ice area immediately. A decision was made to begin a decent at six miles from the airport. There should be no mountains to run into by this point, if only he could get there without running into one.

Oh, oh, the airspeed was dropping. The airplane must be climbing too steeply. No, that couldn't be, the artificial horizon indicated the airplane was straight and level and not climbing at all. It was descending! There must be too much ice on the wings to allow a climb with this power setting. The throttle and the mixture control were fire walled and the prop was adjusted to full fine. This developed the maximum horsepower the engine was capable of developing.

By increasing the horsepower to maximum, the airplane leveled off. Altitude could be maintained, but the airplane would not climb! The air speed began to drop. Too much ice must have accumulated on the wings and maneuvering was becoming sluggish.

The speed of the airplane slowed to just above the stall speed and it was necessary to hold the nose high in order to maintain altitude. Even a shallow turn would almost certainly stall the airplane. The situation was getting more desperate and more desperate. Something was going to have to be done immediately to improve the condition of the airplane.

The engine started to run rough. The air intake was quickly closed so the engine would breathe warm air from inside the cowling, rather than outside air. Ice must be building up in the air intake.

The air speed indicator went to zero. Ice must be covering the pitot tube. The Pitot heat was turned on. Flight characteristics of the airplane were diminishing rapidly.

The engine continued to run rough and the airplane was unable to maintain altitude and began to descend. Several minutes went by before the running of the engine improved. The ice in the air intake must have thawed from the warmer air entering the fuel injector and the engine came back to full life.

The prop was cycled from full fine to full pitch, and then back again to full fine. Some of the ice was thrown off. The airplane was still descending but the rate of decent had slowed a little by loosing some of the ice. The airplane had lost elevation and was now down to 4,000 feet. How high were those mountains in this area?

Upon reaching 8.4 miles from Crest Airpark, the airplane had lost another 100 feet to 3,900. Pattern altitude was 1,500 feet. If the airplane can descend out of this icing condition and continue to fly, a further descent would be made to 1,500 feet.

Suddenly there was a loud bang. What was that? It must have been the landing gear dropping as the pitch of the airplane changed. The airspeed slowed. The airplane must have been flying near the stall speed because the controls were now mushy. The GPS indicated the ground speed had reduced to 70 knots, just above stalling speed.

The automatic landing gear drop system must have dropped the gear as the airplane slowed. Either the pitot tube, which controls this system, was plugged with ice, or the automatic gear drop system activated due to the low speed of the airplane.

The gear was raised and locked in place so the automatic gear drop system would not activate.

How long was this going to last? The airplane began to vibrate and had become nearly uncontrollable due to the ice. Still nothing could be seen out the windows. Somehow, some of this ice had to be shaken loose or melted or the airplane would literally fall out of the sky.

The GPS indicated Crest Airpark was 6.2 nautical miles away. Hopefully the airplane had flown out of the mountainous area enough to descend. The altitude indicator indicated 3,500 feet. The airplane was stuck in a gentle descent created by the ice building up and could not be turned without fear of stalling. Level flight could not be maintained and it was impossible to climb. The rate of descent was increased sharply in hope of getting to lower and warmer air faster.

Distance to Crest was now 4.3 nautical miles and the altitude was down to 3,000 feet, still descending in the thick fog. Little by little, visibility out the front began to improve. The end of the wings could be seen. It was not a good sight. The leading edges of the wings were covered with an inch of ice and there must have been hundreds of pounds on other parts of the airplane.

Another bang was heard. What was that? It must have been some of the ice coming off the front of the airplane and hitting the top of the fuselage. The airplane had to be flown lower into warmer air.

It seemed like an eternity since the airplane had entered the fog. Never before had John witnessed flying so frightening and he had turned white with fear.

Somehow the wings were going to have to be kept level. Critical attention must be made of the artificial horizon and other instruments on the dash board. The RPM must also not be allowed to build too fast. This would indicate the airplane was descending too fast in a dive. John began to talk to himself out loud, "Calm yourself and think!"

If 1,500 feet had been reached and the airplane had still not broken out into the clear, Seattle Flight Service would be called, and an emergency would be declared. Up until that point John was too busy trying to fly the airplane to call anyone on the radio. Perhaps they could guide the flight to a different airport, providing the airplane was still flyable.

All of a sudden a glimpse of the ground appeared about 1000 feet below. Then the airplane popped out the bottom of the fog, into the clear.

Wow! What a relief this was. John must have been holding his breath because he suddenly exhaled about ten pounds of air.

Great care still had to be taken. John glanced at the outside air temperature gage and found out the air temperature was now above freezing. The airplane was still descending and, although conditions had improved considerably, there was still a major problem on John's hands. The airplane seemed to be completely covered with what must have been several hundred pounds of ice. Maintaining altitude was still impossible. Something must be done to shed some of this ice.

John cycled the landing gear. This didn't seem to do any good as most of the ice was on the leading edge surfaces of the wings and the forward part of the fuselage. In fact by cycling the gear, John realized he had done the wrong thing. This slowed the airplane down even more and the rate of descent increased. There was only about a thousand feet left to play with, so a solution had to be worked out, or there was serious trouble coming his way.

The flaps were cycled several times. This broke loose a little of the ice, but not enough to do much good. It did, however, slow the rate of decent down a little by creating more lift. The flaps were left down at 5 degrees, the first level, to create as much lift as possible, without adding too much drag. Lowering beyond this would add drag and slow the airplane even more, increasing the descent.

What more could be done to shed this ice? The airplane was flying in above freezing level temperature, but enough weight from the ice had to be lost to be able to maintain level flight. The airplane would have to remain in this temperature a great deal longer for the ice to melt enough to allow the airplane to fly normally.

Movement of the airplane through the air was working against him. It was tending to cool, rather than warm the exposed surfaces.

The ground was coming ominously closer and closer. Flight continued west where the land descends from the mountains to sea level. This would gain at least another 600 feet. The lower the airplane went, the higher the temperature was becoming, one degree at a time.

What else could be done to slow the rate of descent? The prop was cycled again. As the prop control lever was pulled back, the pitch changed. Ice began to peal off in small chunks. The prop was cycled several times more and then the pitch was set to full fine to increase the horsepower back to maximum.

This helped considerably, but the airplane would still not fly level, nor would it climb. Without better control, an attempt to land was out of the question. The emergency channel 121.5 was called and an emergency was declared.

John: "May day! May Day! May Day! Cherokee 8475 Charlie. I am iced up and descending".

Air Controller: "8475 Charlie. Squawk seven seven zero zero. What is your location and altitude?"

John changed the transponder from squawking 1200 to 7700.

John: "75 Charlie. I am 5.8 miles West of Crest Airpark at 900 feet descending at 100 feet per minute."

Air Controller: "75 Charlie. Can you make it to Crest Airpark?

John: "Negative. I have little lateral control of the airplane and can not make a turn without stalling."

Air Controller: "75 Charlie. What is your intention?"

John: "I am in warmer air and loosing some ice. I am attempting to get to lower ground. I am directly in line with Commencement Bay, and will attempt to reach sea level for a little more room under me."

Air Controller: "75 Charlie. Proceed. We will try to get you some help."

After another eternity, Commencement Bay was reached and the airplane flew out over the waters of Puget Sound, near Tacoma. By this time, a little distance had been gained between the airplane and the ground, or water as it had now turned out to be. There was less than 500 feet between the bottom of the airplane and the water, and the airplane was still descending. John was near panic.

If a water landing had to be made, He would keep the airplane as close to the shore as possible. The water temperature in the Sound was about 50 degrees. If the airplane bellied in, and he came out alive, there would only be a few minutes available for him to swim to shore. The cold temperature of the water would soon lower the body temperature, and create other trouble.

John: "75 Charlie, I am loosing a little ice as I go. My rate of decent is now 50 feet per minute and I am gaining some lateral control."

Air Controller: "75 Charlie, Can you fly down the Kent Valley to Renton Airport?"

John: "75 Charlie, negative. There is a hill between the Kent Valley and me. I am now over Commencement Bay, near Tacoma."

Air Controller: "We have you on radar now. Are your instruments operable?"

John: "75 Charlie, My air speed indicator is out, but everything else is working."

Air Controller: "75 Charlie, turn to a heading of two niner seven. We will bring you into Sea-Tac."

John: "What elevation is Sea-Tac?"

Air Controller: "75 Charlie, Sea-Tac elevation is zero four two niner. Make a right turn to zero two zero."

John: "75 Charlie, my rate of decent is too fast. I can't make it to zero four two nine. I will be too low by the time I get there. I will continue across the water until the ice melts. I am loosing ice faster and the airplane is becoming more responsive."

Air Controller: "75 Charlie, proceed. We will bring you into Whidbey Island. Elevation zero niner zero. Turn left to three two five. Expect a new bearing in five minutes."

The prop was frantically cycled again. Little ice came off this time, but the surge up and down of the air speed must have shaken loose some of the ice on the wings and body. A loud bang was heard on the top and bottom of the fuselage. The water was getting closer.

A few small pieces of ice flew off the wings into the air. Then a larger piece must have dropped off because another loud bang was heard.

By this time the airplane was almost skimming across the top of the water. If complete control couldn't be gained in a minute or so, John was going to be in the water. He was nearly frantic. The water looked mighty cold. There was only a few more feet left below the airplane.

Another large chunk of ice seemed to come off, then another. The descent rate slowed to zero and John pulled the control column back a little more. Caution had to be taken to keep from pulling back too hard on the controls. If this happened, the airplane could easily stall, critical altitude could be lost, and the airplane could be in the water. John pulled the control column back very gently to test his ability to climb the airplane. The airplane began to rise just a little.

The throttle was pushed again, as if it was not already fire walled. A large chunk of ice must have fallen off as the airplane jumped up in the air with a sudden surge. It was now a race to loose ice and weight and gain lift and airspeed. At least level flight could be maintained, and with caution a gentle climb could be made. A turn could only be made at a shallow angle. Pulling back on the control column was still extremely dangerous. The warmer air would have to do its job before the airplane could be flown anywhere over land.

Bang! There went a lot more ice. Chunks could be seen lifting off the upper wing surface. The airplane was beginning to fly a little better. Level flight could be maintained without having the nose of the airplane raised.

Several minutes went by as more ice came off the airplane. Flight continued at this low altitude to take advantage of the warmer temperature close to the water."

The flight characteristics of the airplane improved slowly over the next half-hour. Climbing and maneuvering became possible, so the nose was raised and the airplane was pointed back toward Crest Airpark. Crest was now nearly 40 miles away.

John: "75 Charlie, I just dropped a large load of ice and am able to climb."

Air Controller: "That's good news 75 Charlie. What is your intention?"

John: "75 Charlie, the airplane is responding well. I will cancel the emergency and return to Crest."

Air Controller: "Ga' day, 75 Charlie. We will monitor your progress."

John: "Thanks for the help! 75 Charlie."

Approaching within 15 miles of Crest, the radio was tried in an attempt to reach Crest Unicom. There was no answer. There must not have been anyone at the FBO (Fixed Base Operator) office, or the antenna on the airplane was still covered with ice. Thank God the GPS was still working.

The airplane climbed to pattern altitude and the airport was flown over. Several inches of snow could be seen on the runway and it had not been plowed. John was near total exhaustion. The sun had sunk below the horizon in the west and the visibility was rapidly diminishing.

A decision was made to land at Crest even though the snow appeared quite deep. If an alternate airport were chosen, a landing would have to be made in the dark. A night landing on a strange airport in his exhausted condition could be even more dangerous than landing in the snow.

John entered the pattern and a soft field landing was planned to keep from tipping the airplane over as the snow caught the landing gear. The flaps and landing gear were lowered and the power was cut back. The nose was raised and the airspeed was lowered to 80 MPH. The nose was raised even higher and the power was increased in order to hold the airplane at 70 MPH, just above stalling. Over the threshold of the runway the airplane was stalled completely and the airplane sank gently onto the runway, nose high.

The main gear touched first and the nose gear remained in the air momentarily and then came down with a loud bang. The airplane came to a sudden stop without having to use the brakes. The snow decelerated the airplane fast and the nose gear came down with an abrupt thud. Perhaps not one of his whisper landings, but he was down and safely on the ground.

What can be said after this? John thought about kissing the ground. Whoever said, "It is better to be on the ground, wishing you were in the air, rather than in the air, wishing you were on the ground"? How prophetic!

John's Notes: Few of us have bargained with the "Ice Machine" and have come through unscathed. Some do's and don'ts have been developed as a result of this incident. Firstly, be cognoscente the "Ice Machine" can exist during either winter or summer when the freezing level is below 10,000 feet. Secondly, when flying in close proximity to the mountains, never attempt to fly under low hanging clouds or fog, particularly when either flying up and over the mountains, or when flying over and down the mountains. Thirdly, when flying up or down a valley to cross the mountains, always fly to one side leaving enough room to turn around. If low clouds or fog are about to be encountered, make an immediate 180 in the room left to one side of the valley. Fourthly, when fog or low clouds are encountered, circle to gain altitude into clear air before climbing over the mountains. When descending, always remain over the top of clouds or fog until reaching close to your destination. Generally, this can be done in clear air. Fifthly, never, never bargain with the "Ice Machine"!